JACK THE BEAR

Books by Dan McCall

Dan McCall

JACK THE BEAR

Doubleday & Company, Inc., Garden City, New York, 1974

All of the characters in this book are fictitious,
and any resemblance to actual persons, living
or dead, is purely coincidental.

ISBN: 0-385-02545-9
Library of Congress Catalog Card Number: 73–10809
Copyright © 1974 by Dan McCall
All Rights Reserved
Printed in the United States of America
First Edition

This book belongs to Steven

I acknowledge with gratitude the generous
support of the John Simon Guggenheim Memorial Foundation.

JACK THE BEAR

"The secret of my success with children," Dad always says, "is that they think I'm one of them." Lots of adults when they play with you you can tell they'd really rather be doing something else, but Dad forgot to grow up. That's why he was so good on KID STUFF, his TV show. He's still good, but not like before. Obviously. It's because of another thing he said, which was this, "All I want to do with my life is stay home and fuck my wife and play with my boys." Well, he still can play with John, Jr. (which is me, Jack, Jack The Bear), and with Dylan my brother, who is 3, but he never ever again will be able to fuck his wife, Mom, because she died last winter. And they had been separated, not divorced, but separated for almost a year. So now instead of going back and forth between houses in Syracuse NY, it's Dad and Dylan and me in this one in Oakland CA.

When Mom and Dad first started having big trouble, back in Syracuse, I blamed myself, and Dylan of course, because some of their fights were about us, but Dad explained to me that all kids blame themselves when their parents are having a rough time. It's a common reaction. Still, I used to be pretty horrible to Dylan in Syracuse when I saw him hassling them, even though I knew it wasn't our fault. And it wasn't anybody's fault when she died, unless maybe hers, being out on icy roads at 3 o'clock in the morning. But I can't stop the nightmares. And neither can Dad. Sometimes when I wake up sweating, and go downstairs for a glass of milk, he's already there. Or vice versa. And then we talk a little or just sit there at the dining-room table. He has brandy or coffee or both. We watch the darkness get gray and hear the *Chronicle* hit the front door.

You have to go on living, you have to pull yourself together. Dad has his work. In Syracuse it was Channel 44, and here in Oakland it's Channel 2. He's taken me to the studio a couple of times, but I didn't get to be on the show like before. Dad doesn't even have a show of his own, he is the Monster of Ceremonies on Thriller. He does have a show on radio, though, which is also called KID STUFF again, and I got to do a Northridge Bread commercial for that, but we did it at home on tape. Dylan's on it too, he just says "MORE BREAD" at the top of his lungs at the last moment. Sometimes Dad passes out after taping because he's so worried about jobs and bringing up his boys on his own and the whole situation and his sadness for Mom. He's very lonely. He blows too much dope, and he even drinks. One night when I found him downstairs crashed on the couch he was crying, really crying in his sleep, and it was worse because Dylan had the flu and a temperature of 103. That surprised us, we didn't even know about it, we just went for a routine check-up. The Nurse was all shocked and freaked-out and said, "This child has a fever of 103." Dad was completely shook up, because all we knew the night before was that Dylan lay down on the couch all beat and kind

12

of slow, which is unusual for him. We never felt the fever, and we never took his temperature because Dad broke the thermometer weeks ago, it just sailed out of his hand into a thousand pieces. In the Doctor's office I knew he was feeling that he was a shitty father, but there was nothing I could say. I mean, I can't say, "Don't worry, you're not a shitty father." Besides, Dylan got over it in 2 days.

Dad's first thought in coming here, of course, was to get away from the painful memories. But he also belongs out here in the Bay Area for several reasons. One obvious one is he has connections. They were even talking about it, Mom and Dad, at the time of the separation, and before. Dad is a college graduate from San Francisco State, in Theatre Arts and Communication. I talked with one of his old professors at that cocktail party Dad had here when I served the stuff on trays and took orders for refills and had a bad case of being cute. I was just imitating. Dad was sweating and wearing his favorite flower-power shirt and his orange bellbottoms and his boots, and being a little spectacular. I know he was putting on an act, but sometimes that's what you have to put on. Especially now.

The house we've rented is "bad." Which means good. Dad calls it The Pink Fang, because it's tall (3 stories) and thin and pink and old. The man who built it in 1921 was an architect, and took tender loving care (TLC) especially because his wife couldn't walk, she was a paralyzed invalid, and he had her problem in mind when he was doing it. For example, there are bells like doorbells in all the rooms where in days gone by she could wheel herself up and signal. When the three of us play the flashlight game at night, one of us is always ringing, or all three of us ring—like maybe I'm in the basement and Dad's hunting around with the flashlight, we turn off all the lights so that it's pitch-dark, and Dylan is hiding in his bedroom closet. Dylan doesn't really get the idea of the game—like if you call out, "Wheeeeere's Dylan?" he'll tell you, he'll just pipe up, "He's in a closet."

We also play outside, in the daylight, usually in the twilight, after school before dinner, with the kids in the neighborhood. They won't give Dad a moment's peace. He's always been a madman for playing with kids—and even though it could sound weird to some people he's even more so now after all the heartbreak. Like he *has* to do it. I'm probably the only one who knows how much, because I see him afterward, and I know how much of himself he puts into it. But other kids just think he's Super Weirdo, and they giggle themselves into fits. Every afternoon around 4:30 they all come over and ask, "When is the Monster coming out?" Dad sometimes puts on his TV make-up, and then he's one of his favorite disguises, Caesar Asparagus, and he chases everybody. Mrs. Festinger, Edward's mother, caught us on the sidewalk and she said to Dad, "What is this strange power you have over children?" I thought Dad was going to say what he always says, about being a big-one-of-them, but this time he said, "I am a perfect monster." And he is. He robots around saying, "I want to eat a kid, want to eat a kid," and his face is green-blue, and everybody's laughing and scared, and his voice goes way down like it's in the basement of the whole world, "Eat A Kid, EAT A KID," and he says, "you are a dingaling, and you are a meshuggener, I'll hang you by the thumbs." Edward, who is slightly retarded and has a pie face, actually did hang himself by the thumbs, temporarily, on a pole. And then Dad will suddenly stop and be calm and say, "Let's all try to be adult about this. I don't see any monsters. The Monster only appears when there is a metal light in the sky." And then he is just like any other adult, all relaxed and bored, until somebody says, "Look, what's that? Up in the sky, it's an airplane, it's a helicopter." And Dad will say,

"What? I don't see any—" and he'll stop short, and turn slowly, and begin to change slowly and gradually, like poor old Larry Talbot, into the Wolfman, and we all go flying in all directions and somebody not meaning to runs over Dylan and we have to stop while Dad kisses where he hurt himself and dries his tears.

The real problem is the dogs. The people in back of us, facing the other street, Carmichael, they raise Dobermans and they've got about 10 of them, and sometimes they go crazy gnashing their teeth and howling and barking. Everybody's complained about it, but it's not a commercial business, like a kennel, so what can you do? It's their hobby. For us it is a shame because our back yard is a perfect monster arena, it slides downhill for twenty yards that's never been cared for, at least not in years, all ivy and spooky moss trees and stuff that I call wolfbane. You can creep through it, because there are ivy and lacy tunnels, it must have run wild since 1921 or since World War II. But now if we get into heavy Monsterism, the dogs go into their act. One of them got through a hole in the fence, and it was pretty lucky for all concerned that he was a puppy—he'd just had his ears trimmed and set, with splints and bandages, it looked like he had miniature goal posts on his head, complete with the crossbar. Dylan never used to be afraid of dogs, but he is now, he's petrified. The dogs bark even when nobody's there, like at sunrise, which drives everybody out of their tree. That's why Dad restricts his Monsterism mostly to the front yard, which isn't even in the running. Sometimes I play with Dylan very quietly in the back because there is an enormous tree, it must be fifty feet high, with moss fixed in free of charge. It is one noble tree, and the people who owned the house at one time put a tree house in it where I go up on several occasions to smoke one of Dad's joints (he doesn't count them).

I want to make one thing perfectly clear, which Dad

15

says as a joke. It's not. It is this, the thing doesn't always finish happy, after the Monster comes out. One day Dad was boozed and really kind of out of control. He tripped and fell down and broke his rose-colored sunglasses, and then Katy, Edward's sister who isn't retarded, said, "I smell something on your breath, and I know what it is." Dad slowed down and said, "What?" and Katy shouted, "WHISKEY!" Dad turned pale and went into the house. Even I know it wasn't whiskey, it was gin. That was the night he threw up on the spaghetti.

It was also the night I had one of my worst dreams about Mom. In the dream we were in the old house in Syracuse, and she was sitting on my bed in the middle of the night, as she did so many times, smoothing the hair back from my forehead, and she was saying, "Jacky Bear, will you always love your mother? Will you always?" And I woke up screaming YES. She was always afraid we didn't love her enough. You simply couldn't convince her. I remember at the funeral, the last time I saw her, I had only one thought in my mind, to convince her. I would have done anything, and in one dream I made it, and she was only the Sleeping Princess, and my kiss broke the spell of death. One of the things that upsets me the most in my dreams is that fucking idea of a *second chance*. I'd gladly give up my own life to have that, which is what you're supposed to say, but I mean it. No questions asked.

One thing I'm learning now is that everybody in the whole world has really terrible problems. Dexter's mother came over one day while we were playing Monsterism. She is not really Dexter's mother, we know that, she's his grandmother—his real mother and father split, they split from each other and they split from him, they split from everything. Mom and Dad at their worst never did that. Dexter's mother is in reality his grandmother, and sometimes when I think that our situation is hopeless I just think about what Dexter's dealing with and what he has to look forward to. He's not loved by anybody, not really *loved*. His mother is in fact up in the world only 4 hours a day, and his grandmother anyway, and his father, which is his grandfather, is about as bad except that he can hold down a job. She is completely passed out from pills and booze from dawn to dusk, he is passed out from dusk to dawn. Dad says they're members of Alcoholics Monogamous.

Which is why the parents along our street won't let their kids go to the Mitchell house to play. Edward broke his right arm over there last year, and one month later Katy broke her left arm in the back yard. Some people say it was just a coincidence, but Mr. Festinger, their father —Dad calls him Earthquake McGoon, because he's muscle-bound and works out with dumbbells—said, "When they both had those casts on, I said, 'I've had it.'" Dexter gets the blame, but he wouldn't mean to do it. He just can't listen. You tell him something in the huddle when we're playing touch football, and when the ball is hiked he does something completely different. He also keeps running blindly into things at full speed like our hedge.

Anyway, Mrs. Mitchell came over, walking all stiff and holding onto little pieces of the hedge to keep steady, and she said to Dad, "I bring you neighborly warning." Dad stopped being Caesar Asparagus, and they went up to the porch, but I heard it all when I was hiding down there by the blue wading pool which we got a lot of use out of in August, horsing around. I sat on the hose coiled up like a serpent. Mrs. Mitchell talked about Norman, who is the neighborhood problem. Norman is waiting for the express to Barf City. He lives directly across the street from us in a fat house—Dad says we live in The Pink Fang and Norman & Company (his parents) live in the Green Molar. On the back of Norman's jacket it says, KILLER

17

BY DAY, LOVER BY NIGHT. When Dad first met him, Dad said, "Got the time?" Norman is completely messed up. He is about 30, and he's a white dude except that his skin color is all gray and hopeless, like a dead campfire. He walks with a cane that kids say has a hidden sword in it, he just walks and walks around the block like he is on Guard Duty, and every day at a quarter to nine when everybody's going to school Norman washes his old orange '59 Thunderbird which is parked so that we can't get into our driveway without pulling up in front of the Mitchells' and then backing up into the driveway of the Green Molar and then coming back down into our own, which usually takes Dad a couple of tries and a few goddamits and shits. When Norman washes his orange T-Bird some of the kids lob clods or even rocks at him, and when he chases you it is not Monsterism, he'd probably rape you. But the only trouble Norman has given us was not heavy, just two things. One is his big white dog, Cheyenne, that dumps in our yard every morning. The other is when he cut his foot real bad and Dad drove him to the hospital. Norman must not have a variety of friends if he had to ask us, when we had just moved in and were strangers. His stupid foot bled all over the gold carpet in the front seat of our Dodge Swinger, and we can't get the stain out, it's permanent, and it reminds you if you don't overlook it.

While I was hiding down there in the dirt by the porch I heard Mrs. Mitchell telling Dad all about Norman's history. Then she went home to crash. Dexter had a cheese sandwich at our house, and then he went home too—he asked me to come in, and I did, and I got scared because there was a body on the sofa and it was her. Dexter tapped her hard right on the forehead with his bare knuckles and he said, "Guess who's here? We've got company." She didn't wake up, she just turned a little. There was a tape recorder machine upstairs, on Play, and I could hear it from where I was, it was Dexter's bedtime story. I know when it's time to leave, so I left.

I'm always scared now. I have a bad habit of hearing things, like somebody small and far away and forlorn and crying. It's Mom, of course. We have lots of pictures, and I look at them, the snapshots of happy days that Dad took, where I'm a baby, and where Dylan's a baby, and the week in Maine, and whole chapters in photographs of when we were One Big Happy Family. And Mom's college graduation portrait, in a gold frame. I stare and stare and make up conversations. I have visions of when they were dating, or when they went horseback riding (which they probably never did). And there toward the end, in the late afternoon when you couldn't see out to the street because of the sheets of snow, Mom saying, "I've got to be my-self again." She knew what was happening to everything, but she didn't have the strength. Nobody can ever tell me she didn't try with all her heart because I know how hard she did. The night she died she probably just saw she would never make it. She couldn't conquer her fears.

I'm trying to conquer mine. The old ones and the new ones. The new ones are like here in The Pink Fang when I'm upstairs in our house and I can look straight across the street and see Norman at his window, sitting there and thinking about everything and watching whatever only his own eyes can see. He has a gun. I try to keep my distance. Dylan calls Norman "Big Trouble." Dylan has developed a fear of dogs and Norman. All the ancient history I know about Norman is that he had a bumper sticker on his '59 orange T-Bird once that said SEGREGA-TION FOREVER, because he hates black people. There were a lot of complaints about that, as bad as about the Dobermans. People, mainly blacks, painted things on the house and the concrete steps, which in spite of paint remover you can still see, especially the sign which Dad told me is a swastika, for Nazis. Now Norman just has a bumper sticker that says WALLACE, which is useless because Wallace was shot and can't run. Like the '59 T-Bird which can't move. In our neighborhood it's 99 per cent MC GOVERN stickers and signs, and two NIXON stickers on two cars that belong to one family and old Crazy Norman's one WALLACE. I can tell he hates my long hair.

Mostly I'm scared at night, when Dad's at the studio. I watch him do the commercials on Thriller, so in one way he is home, in Living Color, but I leave it on for the Late Late Show until I hear the Dodge Swinger, and then I snap off our new Zenith and fly to bed. He caught me once, but he was good about it. The sitter he hired through an agency, Alice, was ridiculous, and he's looking for somebody else.

Dad is like Avis, he tries harder. He is good about almost anything, and never gets mad. Lots of people would get mad about things he doesn't. Like he told me a story about how he had lunch one day at a Mexican Restaurant on Telegraph Avenue in Berkeley, and in the middle of the meal he found out the water pitcher was empty, so he took it back to the kitchen and got it filled up, and then he came back to the table and there was this street-people hippie sitting there eating the rest of Dad's lunch. Dad wasn't mad at all, he just laughed. When he told me the whole story he did an imitation of the hippie. "Oh, man, like wow, you weren't finished? Man, I'm like sorry." You simply cannot get Dad mad. He has always had a theory of Downward Mobility. He was monstering for us the other day and a cute little black kid named Ray peeked up over the corner of our gold Swinger, and Ray said to Dad, "Monster, you fulla shit!" Dad smiled and said, "Right on!" and turned around to eat somebody else.

Dylan goes to the Kinder Haus Nursery School five days a week, and I go to the Piedmont Experimental School where I am a Roving Reporter for The *Piedmont Experimental School Tattler* (THE PEST), and I want to be a journalist someday. The kids are all right, but I haven't developed relationships with my own age group, and I run with younger kids who look up to me or at least don't compete. You have to wait when you're new in town, and self-conscious. One girl actually thinks that speed and grass and acid are something people in Alaska take. I don't know where she got that idea. I'm doing a series in THE PEST about adventures in Guacamole, New Mexico, the scene of the rampage of the Taco Bats, and Dad types them for me on his ROYAL. He gave me a Bullitzer Brize, a gold cut-out star on a blue ribbon which I wear around my neck. There's also a certificate signed by the Associated Daughters of Motel Operators.

Yesterday we were playing touch football in the street while Crazy Norman was sitting up in the ivy on his private property, NO TRESPASSING, wearing his jacket with the printing KILLER BY DAY, LOVER BY NIGHT, and throwing rocks at Cheyenne, who was tied up. Dad was upset because Dexter said to him he had gray hairs, and Dad went into the house to see in the mirror. When he came out he said it was totally untrue and false, "an accusation without foundation in fact," and then Dexter found one and Dad had me pull it out and show it to him. He had to face the evidence. It hurt. Dylan is not allowed in the street, and Dad spanked him hard once when he went, so my kid brother was our cheering section on the sidewalk. The only cheer he knows is "Go, Man, Go!" He also says "MORE BREAD!" Dexter as usual didn't know what to do, but Dad lets us take turns calling a series, so Dexter says in the huddle, "You pass it to me, and I'll pass it to you for a home run—K?" and he says the K real hard, pounding his palm with his finger, and then the ball comes to him and he runs blindly full speed into the hedge again. He can't think straight. On defense he says to me, "You take the black guy," which is stupid because *both* guys on their line are black. Dad went out on one play and I threw a pass to him which Michael, who can really run, intercepted. Dad tried to grab him and fell down. Mr. Festinger Earthquake McGoon across the street, who was bringing down the garbage, laughed in a nasty way at Dad and said, "You got outmaneuvered, Superstar." Some people I don't like, but Mr. Festinger I don't like almost as much as Norman. Mr. Festinger has pork-chop mutton-chop sideburns, and he says, "Gimme five, Tiger," and tries to be a Far-Out Adult in the Now Generation, but he is also into very stupid muscle building for trophies and screams at his slightly retarded son, old Edward, and I saw him slap him once on the face, really hard. Dad spanks Dylan and me maybe a grand total of 8 times per year but he never slaps on the face. Mr. Festinger is one of the people Norman attacked years ago with a branch of a tree. Cheyenne likes to take dumps on Mr. Festinger's yard too, Cheyenne is the champ dumper of the neighborhood, and Mr. Festinger says if it does not stop pronto he'll kill that goddamn dog with poison. But maybe Norman will kill the dog first, throwing rocks at him, he's already put out Cheyenne's left eye. It looks like a dead marble.

Anyway Dad was really enjoying running around shouting things like "Good play, good play" and "Blitz" and giving Michael holy hell when he played Superfly and said "Oh sheeyyyit" like black dudes do and punched out Dexter for holding. Dad penalized Michael half the distance to the fire plug for unsportsmanlike conduct, personal foul, and poopersville. Then we all had an apple juice break on the porch and Dexter wanted to know when the monster would reappear, and Dad said he was fagged out. But Dylan said, over and over, "I want a monster, I want a monster," so finally Dad bowed to popular demand and looked at the metal light in the sky and changed into Marcus Superfluous. He robot-walked and chanted, "Eat A Kid! EAT A KID!" and Katy came over through the Secret Passage, which is merely a hole in the hedge, and she went after Dad. She said, "Eat a Grown-Up! EAT A GROWN-UP!" and then Henry Abrams from the end of the street came by on his unicycle. There was a cardboard sign on the back of Henry's unicycle, taped between the wheel and the seat, his parents made it and it said in red printing

ANOTHER UNICYCLE
FOR MC GOVERN

Dad really liked that, and he rode the unicycle a little because he's been riding unicycles for years and years before I was even born. He was a clown in the Clyde Beatty Circus. I can ride them too of course because Dad has taught me everything he knows. I'll never forget when we moved into The Pink Fang in August and Henry

Abrams came by to show off for the new neighbors and I pretended to be impressed and asked him if I could try, and he said no, and I said, "I'll bet you a quarter I can ride it if you give me 3 tries, it doesn't look so hard," and Henry laughed and said, "Let's see your money," so then he handed the uni to me and I pedaled off into the sunset while his jaw completely dropped. I didn't take the quarter because he had no way of knowing my background and what he was getting into. Dad has taken hours of his time to teach me how to do a lot of his old circus tricks and I can do back flips from cartwheels and running forward flips. I can walk on my hands as long as I want to. Once when the Clyde Beatty Circus came to Syracuse Dad went down there and renewed old friendships and he gave Clyde Beatty a lot of free plugs on KID STUFF on Channel 44, and so they let him be his old clown again for one performance at night, and Dad announced it on KID STUFF, and he had to sign autographs and everything because he was a local celebrity, and I was part of the act. I pretended to annoy him and be a royal nuisance, like stealing his derby hat, and he chased me all over the place and so did 2 other clowns. I was just dressed in my regular school clothes, so nobody would suspect, and then I started my cartwheels and back flips and handsprings, and stole a unicycle, which means I stole the whole show, and Dad came after me on a 7-foot uni with a chain drive, and when it was all over we bowed in the spotlight, holding hands, we were SYRACUSE'S OWN, a father and son, and it was simply the high point of my whole fucking life. You can't imagine how it felt, and I can barely remember it. Only totally. Those were the great years.

Now I only say it was a thrill I'll never forget, and I can never thank him enough. In the car on the way home Mom didn't say anything, but she and I both saw that Dad had tears in his eyes. He was feeling the old feeling again. I guess I would like to join the circus, but Dad says the circus is dying and so there is no future in it. But it has given me some valuable training that I can put to use in other fields.

Meanwhile in Oakland Dad was fooling around with Henry Abrams' ANOTHER UNICYCLE FOR MC GOVERN, but Dexter was feeling neglected, and he shouted real loud, "I'M ANOTHER KARATE EXPERT FOR NIXON," and he kept going "Ha-YA!" at Dad with his hands and also with his cowboy boots. Dad caught him by one boot and held him upside down, and Dad told him he was too young to vote for Nixon, moreover he was too young to die, and Dexter was laughing, laughing silly, but when he got free he said, "I hate you." He didn't really mean it, he was just laughing, but Dad said, "Don't say that, Dexter," and Dexter just said it again, loud. Dad said, "I told you not to say that, Dexter," and then Dexter couldn't back down. Dad had already turned away, and old Dylan put up his finger and said to Dad, "I hate you." He didn't mean it either, he was just repeating what he had heard. Dad turned back again to Dexter and said, "Don't ever say that again, Dexter, because there will be plenty of time for Dylan to learn that word, and I don't want him to learn it now." There was a heavy silence. Dexter was swallowing and blinking his eyes and blushed and frantic, and he was swinging his head around the way he does when he is upset and he said, "ANOTHER KARATE EXPERT FOR NIXON," and he ran up and kicked Dad real hard right in the balls.

That's when I gave Dexter a bloody nose. I knew there would be trouble, but I couldn't help myself. Dexter ran home crying and Dad was sitting on the porch trying to catch his breath, and then finally here comes Mrs. Mitchell out of their house, and she's all shaky and holding onto the little pieces of the hedge, her face even redder than usual, and she said to Dad, "My son tells me your son gave him a bloody nose."

Dad still wasn't quite over being kicked in the balls. He was sitting down. He said, "Jack will be disciplined."

I looked at them. I looked at Dylan too, beside Dad, and Dylan was really scared, his eyes all big and round and that blue color which is inherited. Mrs. Mitchell turned on her heels and started navigating her way back to their dump. Then Henry Abrams on his ANOTHER UNICYCLE FOR MCGOVERN, who is a good sport, yelled at her, "He did it because Dexter was teaching the baby to say 'I hate you,' and Dexter kicked Mr. Leary in the crotch." He was pedaling in place, old Henry, gossiping back and forth in place on his uni. Poor Mrs. Mitchell stopped and stood there like a statue for a minute, with her back to us. Then she started going along again, like on rollers. Then she stopped again and turned around and wheeled back to our front walk. She looked at Dad and said, "Is that true?"

Dad got up. He said, "Dexter's high-spirited. It's my fault for playing so rough with them."

Mrs. Mitchell began to cry right there in front of the whole neighborhood. Dad walked her home. She went on crying, and it did not make any sense at all. The rest of us sort of hung around, and Dylan came up with the prize comment of the day, "She crying."

Across the street nobody was crying. Norman was watching.

When things finally calmed down, and we were having dinner, Dad said to me, "I really liked it when you gave Dexter a bloody nose, but don't do it again, K?"

"K," I said, looking at my plate, and then I sneaked a look at him and he was grinning at me.

He changed. "Don't do it again. I mean it."

"I know what you mean," I said proudly.

Later in the evening, though, while Dad was giving Dylan his bath, I answered the doorbell and it was Dexter's father, which is actually his grandfather. Dad pretends to be a Monster but Mr. Mitchell really looks like one, after dark. He's okay when he comes home from work, he gives you a snappy salute. Dexter says his father (grandfather) was a Fighting Seabee and he doesn't have a left wrist, because of a bomb wound, and he can take a plane completely apart and put it back together, just like that, without any parts left over. Well, he comes home and starts with the pills and the booze and his whole face changes. I've seen him twice, he looks even crazier than Norman and his eyes get glassy and he looks like he's carved out of something that froze. He sets his jaw and bites his lip and he asked me if Dad was home. I flew upstairs like something was after me. I took charge of Dylan (actually I just left him, he was playing with his plastic boats and turtle) and listened from the stairs where I was hiding. Mr. Mitchell said, "Did Dexter kick you in the testicles?" Dad went out onto the porch with him and I couldn't hear any more. Dylan splashed me, I got my shirt soaked, and I wanted to spank him, but that would be off limits so I just dried his hair so hard that he cried and I whispered to him, "The pillow, do you want the pillow?" and he knows what that means so he shut up fast.

What the pillow means is that I put it over his face and then lie on it for a minute so he can't breathe. He really gets upset. I do that because I can't spank him. One time I did, and then he showed Dad the fingerprints, and Dad said I couldn't, so that's why I use the pillow instead.

Dad came back in and smoked a joint and then we got Dylan in his pajamas and robe and went down to the basement. Dylan sits on the stool at the net, holding his paddle and ball, saying, "Go, Man, Go," and Dad beat me at ping-pong 21–16. Then we played 10 minutes of the flashlight game, and I got really scared in the laundry room because I had seen *The Thing* on Thriller Theatre and I thought it was coming after me—Dylan's too young to get scared of that, but I get completely petrified. Then Dad did the *In And Out Book* with Dylan. We called it a night. Dad had to go to the studio, and I heard the new sitter come in, Mrs. Sampson. She talked with Dad and I came down and introduced myself. She was old and black and I could see right away she wouldn't let me stay up late to watch Thriller. I decided that next day I'd ask Dad if we could move the TV up to the master bedroom (because then I could sneak in there and watch it with the earphones so she wouldn't know).

Later that night I went down to check and she was asleep. I wandered around. I went out on the roof, the sun deck, but I got afraid of The Thing again. I woke up Dylan and scooted back to bed, but Mrs. Sampson didn't even wake up so I had to give him a drink, and it was all right because I wasn't so scared. He cried and said, "I want Mommy," which he still does every once in a while, so I said she went away, and then I was lonely. I went to my room and played with my clay town, but I really wanted to watch Thriller because it was a good one, *Frankenstein Conquers the World,* which is Japanese, with their foolish imitation monsters, and I thought about Syracuse and KID STUFF when Dad used to end it by saying, "Are you awwll *right,* Jack?" which was our own private signal. He always said that, it was his sign-off.

I thought some more about Mr. and Mrs. Mitchell and how I really nailed Dexter. Then I thought about the time Dad was going after the ping-pong ball that he slammed into the dirt area where the floor stops in the basement and he banged his noggin and knocked himself out for a minute. He was stoned. I tried to pick him up and Dylan was crying as usual and Dad was really beautiful, his face was all smooth, because he had freshly shaved. I was relieved when he woke up and gave himself the "Father of the Year" award. Sometimes at night he cuts pieces of his hair off, and once he shaved his whole chest bare. I was thinking about those things and I must have fallen asleep. But I woke up when he came home because he had a woman with him. I could hear them down there talking, and Mrs. Sampson going away with her money, and then they were talking some more and laughing, and maybe fucking. I hid at the top of the stairs, and Dad was saying that the garages were too small, which was why the cars were parked in the street, and he said that the colors of the houses are avocado instead of green and turquoise instead of blue like colors on TV when the flesh-tone button is off. I don't know why he was talking about colors of houses. I saw her when the woman came up to pee, and she was pretty and tall, much taller than Mom was, and I could smell her perfume after she flushed and went back down. I just can't understand why Dad would tell her about the color of houses.

I got in another fight, the next day at school, during

lunch period—and this was just after Dad had told me not to. Claude Layton who is 3 years older than me threw an apple at me, and I was going to bloody his nose like I did Dexter's, but Claude Layton is a big mother fucker and so I ran home. At lunch period, which is forbidden. When I came into the house, there was a vase on the floor just inside the door, and it had three roses in it and a sign on it with scotch tape that said "UP!" with an arrow. I heard Dad from upstairs, and he said, "Im*medi*ately!" so I went up, and he was lying in his bed without his pajamas on, and you could smell the grass he'd been smoking. He was very surprised to see me. He got up and put on his robe, and we had apple juice in the dining room. While we were talking the lady from the night before came in, and I said I wanted to go back to school. She was even taller than she seemed in the dark wearing bracelets with long red hair.

I didn't go back to school. I knew perfectly well what was going on and I was also pissed off. I went down to Long's and read comics and had a chocolate shake and walked and walked all the way around Lake Merritt. I sneaked into Fairyland from the duckpond and a black kid in the dragon slide said, "I gonna beat ass, mothah-fuckah, you wish you nevah born," and I had had enough fights for a 24 hour period so I sneaked out again over the fence where I came in and walked for miles. I don't know why I even went to fucking Fairyland in the first place. I picked up Dylan at the Kinder Haus Nursery School and told another lie, I said Dad had sent me and that we lived just a couple of blocks away so it was all right. Dylan had made a painting of a purple snake that was rolled up with a rubber band around it. This was 4 o'clock. Dad doesn't go till 5. Marcia, who is always there with her big boobs, was not sure about it, but I made a check mark to show Dylan was signed out and then I walked with him back home. He kept saying,

"Humpback, humpback," and I didn't know what he was talking about until finally he said, "Camel." When he got cranky on the hill I spanked him not really hard so it wouldn't show and he stopped. We played around outside a little in the yard and Dexter came over. He had a big bandage on his wrist where he had cut himself and we looked at that and Dylan peed in the hedge. He got it on his shoes. The gold Dodge Swinger was gone from the driveway. I went inside and called out, "Hello, you all," but the only thing you could see was the smell of the grass. Somebody had moved the vase with the roses onto the piano.

When Dad finally drove up he was obviously upset and he said he wanted to talk to me. He'd already been to the Kinder Haus, which means he knew I'd said that lie. Katy came over on her Roller Derby white skates and Dad asked her to take care of Dylan please for a few minutes. He took me into the house.

He said, "I'm listening."

I couldn't look at him.

"You want to have a lemonade while we talk about it?"

"No, sir."

"Sir? What is this sir bit?"

"Mr. Mitchell says you say sir."

"Well, you don't. And you don't have to salute either."

"I'm sorry."

"Relax, man," he said.

I stood there like a bad boy in a movie, racking my brain, and I said, "I brought home a painting Dylan made. There."

He unrolled the purple snake. He said, "Not bad."

I said, "He's only 3."

Dad said, "I'm going to put it up, down in my Growlery, K?"

"K."

Right on cue Dylan started crying outside so we went

out and Katy was sighing and exasperated because Dylan had fallen down in the Secret Passage and he was all tangled up with one pants leg caught on a root. Dexter showed his cut hand again and then Dad rewound the flesh-colored bandage and Henry came along on his ANOTHER UNICYCLE FOR MC GOVERN and Dad didn't want to be a monster until tomorrow.

At dinner I asked him, "What exactly is fucking?"

He thought for a minute and then he said, "First of all it's just about the most incredible thing in the world."

"You did it with Mom a few times."

"Oh, *several* times."

"Are you starting to do it with that woman here in Oakland too?"

He thought for a long time and looked at his lamb and peas with onions. When he started to say something I knew he was confused and so I butted in and said, "It's none of my business."

He said, "No—no, that's all right," and he started to do it again, but he tripped on his own tongue.

We were both saved by Dylan, who was there in his booster seat, and he said, "Daddy and Jack talking." He wasn't eating, just messing around privately.

I jumped at the chance, and I said, "You're silly."

Dylan said, "You're cute."

I said, "I'm not cute. You're cute."

"No," he said and pointed his finger at me, "you're cute."

"Well," Dad said, "I'm wonderful."

He is. He takes us everywhere. To the Pleasure Faire (where I dunked the swami into the water barrel and also killed a boar in the archery skill—not a real one, a wooden one, Dad called it a Crashing Boar). And to Golden Gate Park where we saw an outdoors drama about the clean Cassamassima, the clean Cockamamey, and the clean Conglomerate, which Dylan didn't understand but laughed at a lot and clapped like always. And to Playland by the beach in its final hour where I went down the slides and Dylan went down between Dad's legs, and I stayed on the JOY WHEEL because I scrunched up at the center but Dad kept getting thrown off mainly because he liked to, he's not basically a competitor. And hiking out on the Sky Trail at Point Reyes where I walked 7.2 miles myself and Dylan took a snooze on Dad's shoulders for a mile, and Dad smoked a joint on the forest trail with the sunlight all in streaks and spots and we thought we heard rushing water far away but it was really the wind in the trees. They are happy days, and Syracuse seems far away, which it is. But sometimes it all rushes back when you least expect it.

The Oakland A's, the Amazin A's, won the pennant, and we stayed glued to the set for all seven games of the series, and on that last fly ball in the bottom of the ninth in the seventh game, Dad and I were on our feet and Dylan was scared and then it was all over, and we were champs, and we went out the front door and firecrackers were going off all over the neighborhood and Dad got into the gold Dodge Swinger and started honking the horn, and I got the noisemakers and Dylan started yelling, "Go, Man, Go!" The next day we went down to Lake Merritt and saw the victory parade and I got autographs from Gene Tenace, Rollie Fingers, and Bert Campaneris in their antique cars, and there were unicycles and Dylan petted Charlie O., the mule. Everybody in Oakland was there. Dad said, "You see, we bring luck wherever we go," and I looked at him and he looked at me and then we were both thinking about why we were here, so we didn't talk for a while and just watched the black chicks in the drill teams who are so much better than white girls it isn't even funny. After it was over Dylan ran around the park firing sliders and curve balls with his ping-pong ball and Dad and I sat there feeling pleased that we were champions of the world. We all did some yoga and came home.

That night Dad and I went to the seven o'clock show in Berkeley to see *Yellow Submarine* again. We didn't take Dylan with us this time because the first time we took him he got bored after ten minutes and just wandered up and down the aisles talking to people, which was okay because they were mostly hippies, but we had to leave in the middle (that was back in Syracuse) and so now in Oakland Dad got a new sitter, and she looked like she was responsible even if she was silly and laughed all the time out of awkwardness. The movie was fantastic and afterward I wanted a milk shake and Dad said okay but let's check on Dylan and so he called home, and when he came back to the table he was shaking his head and upset. He said to me, "Dylan's fine, he's asleep. But that sitter, do you know what she said?"

I said tell me.

Dad said, "I asked her how Dylan was and she laughed and she said, 'Oh, he's dead.'"

"Dead?"

"She thought that was a joke." He sat there and he was pale in the white cold light. "Don't make jokes like that, don't ever," he said.

I said, "You don't need to tell me that."

He said, "I know."

It didn't spoil the evening, but we couldn't finish our shakes.

Thursday afternoons are when I am in charge of picking up Dylan at the Kinder Haus unless it's raining, in which case we have a deal that I call Mr. Archer, who drops him off here at the house, which is 1.3 miles away. Whether it rains or not I call Dad at the studio between 4 and 4:30 to check signals.

So on the Thursday after we won the World Series, I called Dad at four and told him about my day at school blah-blah and it was hard to hear him because the construction crew of East Bay Mud, which is what we call the East Bay *Municipal Utilities District*, is laying a new water line down our street and the big equipment was making an unbelievable noise right in front of our house. Dad was telling me to be extra careful and not let Dylan fall into any holes or climb on any rigs when I brought him home, and I was saying "K, K," and then I thought I could hear a siren and then I knew I could because all the machines stopped. Even Dad could hear it, on his end of the phone.

The men outside were shouting, and then I saw three

36

firemen run by the window of our sunroom, and I told Dad. He got scared and told me to check it out, which I did. I went out the front door to the sidewalk and the firemen had had to run because their truck was way down the street, it couldn't get through because of the new water line and all the rigs which were quiet now with men sitting up in the cabs and men with their steel hats standing around. A young guy I had already talked to a few times, with a blond pony tail, a real strong guy about 20 or 21, was all shook up, and trying to light a cigarette right on our walk. I said to him, "Is there a fire?"

He got his cigarette lighted, and he said, "No, no, it's that woman in there, I couldn't get any life signs."

So I knew Dexter's mother had crashed again, but this was an all-time bummer. And then I saw Dexter, carrying his lunchbox, and walking around in circles and going in all directions. I said, "Dexter, is your mom sick?" And he said, "I don't *know*"—he was spinning around and almost falling down, and his eyes were glassy, and he said, "I don't know, she can't *move*."

Another East Bay Mud guy came over to the one with the pony tail, and I heard them talking. I pretended to be just standing there minding my own business, but I was listening. The young guy was saying, "The kid came home and found her, and he came out crying, so I went in. I couldn't get a pulse. I tried wet cloths. If you move her and break something she can sue." The other man, who was much older, was nodding. "I tried mouth to mouth. Man, there was a square yard of pill bottles in there, and empty booze bottles." He was shaking his head, back and forth, while the other man was shaking his up and down.

I could imagine it, and I wished I could have seen him bending over her bed and giving her mouth to mouth, and the square yard of pills. Only I didn't want to see it at all, at the same time.

And then I remembered that Dad was still in there on the phone, worried that our house was burning up, so I ran back in and told him the firemen came for Mrs. Mitchell, who had no pulse.

When I went back outside the East Bay Mud men were still not working and Dexter was looking all around on our grass like he had lost a nickel. I said to him to come in and have a glass of apple juice, which is what Dad would have done, and he said, "Okay," and so we went in and did that. He took a long drink out of one of Dylan's green plastic cups, and then I did, and he wanted another. He said, "Are you poor?"

I said, "No, we're rich." And that was a lie, so I said, "No, we're not rich and we're not poor."

He said, "You're medium."

I said, "We're medium well." I watched him drinking it so fast, and I said, "Why did you ask me if we were poor?"

"Because," he said, putting the green cup back up on the sink, "if you had more money you could buy more glasses and we could both have our own."

"Oh," I said, "we've got a lot, but they're dirty, so they're in the dishwasher."

"Yeah," he said, "my mom never does the dishes either—" and that made him think about his mom and he said, "I got to go now."

I said, "Want potato chips?" Which are his favorite.

He called from the hall, "Nope," and went back outside.

I followed him. The firemen were coming out of the house, and walking along the sidewalk, and the first fireman, in that black heavy uniform to keep them from burning up, said to the East Bay Mud man, "She's gonna be all right, she's breathing."

And while we were inside Mr. Festinger from across the street, old Earthquake McGoon, had made his entrance on the scene. He said to the fireman, "We're neighbors here, and her husband comes home at six o'clock. What should I tell him?"

And I could tell Mr. Festinger wasn't really trying to help, he was just trying to feel important.

The fireman said, "Tell him she's being taken to Highland Hospital."

Mr. Festinger said, "Is she going to be all right?"

The fireman was walking away. He said, "She'll be under observation."

About three minutes went by and then the big rigs started digging away again and Dexter said to me, "Can I have those potato chips now?" I took him inside and gave them to him and when we went back out again the ambulance from Highland Hospital was coming up from the other end of the street, where the East Bay Mud men hadn't got to yet, and the firemen must have told them to come that way. It was a big Cadillac ambulance, pale blue, with a red light blinking on top. By this time some of the kids who had goofed off on the way home were here—some black and some white and some of them Japanese or Chinese—and they waited around when the hospital men went in with the stretcher because they wanted to see Mrs. Mitchell when she came out. Dexter had dropped his bag of chips on the parkway, and I put it up on the top of the hedge where dogs or kids couldn't get it. Adults, also, were coming out and standing on their porches and women in carpet slippers were sort of walking slowly down the street, pretending not to be looking, but really digging the excitement of having something happen in the neighborhood. I did myself, I'm not superior. I knew she was all right and breathing, and the blanket would not be pulled up over her face, but several people didn't know that. Mr. Festinger's mother, who is old and has a German accent, asked Dexter what was happening, and he said, "My mom has to go to Highland Hospital." Mr. Festinger had disappeared.

The rigs stopped again, and the men got off and put out the DANGER signs with the red flashing lights around the holes in the street that they partially filled in, which means Quitting Time. The construction worker with the pony tail went up to the kids and the dogs and said, "Go on now, see who can run fastest to the corner." Another guy with a big bushy handlebar mustache that had fallen down on one side said, "Don't run 'em over with games, just tell 'em to go home." The one with the pony tail got sad about that, because he was the one who went in there and gave her mouth to mouth, and he didn't like criticism.

The third Festinger—his wife—came up, and she said Dexter could come home with her, but he said no, so we all stood around in the warm sun, and I saw by the old clock on the wall, which is my watch, that in a few minutes I'd have to go down to the Kinder Haus and pick up Dylan. A black guy from East Bay Mud walked down and said, "This is bad."

Mrs. Festinger, not the old one, the younger one, sighed and said, "Yes."

The black guy said, "I asked the driver to back up over there so's we could get on by, but he won't move."

Mrs. Festinger understood they weren't talking about the same thing. She was mad, you could see it in her face.

The black guy said, "I got to get home by quitting time."

Then Mrs. Festinger said, "Some people *work* till quitting time."

The black guy looked at her and said shit under his breath and went back to his car. Mrs. Festinger went after him and demanded to know his name. He got into the car, a blue Pinto, and rolled the windows up and just sat there. Mrs. Festinger came back and said to me and Dexter, "It doesn't matter—he'll be here tomorrow, and I'll call the inspector." Her face was all blotched and her eyelids were blinking fast. She said, "Talking like that to children."

He was talking to *her,* of course, not to children. Some people make me puke.

The stretcher came out empty, and they folded it up. And now *Mr.* Festinger came back from wherever he had disappeared to, maybe to take a whiz, and he had to go into his thing again. "Her husband won't be home for an hour and a half—is someone staying to care for her?"

The driver said, "The husband's been contacted, he's on his way."

And then *Mrs.* Festinger, they're a perfect couple, she said, "Shouldn't you wait until he arrives?"

The driver said, "I haven't left, lady."

Mrs. Festinger had had enough obnoxious comments for one day, and she demanded Dexter go with her, which he did after he got the potato chips I left on the top of the hedge.

Mr. Festinger sort of drifted around the street, smoking, holding his gut in and frowning.

I went into the sunroom for a while, and looked at one of Dad's *Playboys,* and then just sat there having a Nervous trip, and the street out there was like a magnet, so I went outside again. I sat on the curb. After a few minutes Mr. Mitchell drove up in their beat-up Plymouth, looking for a place to park among all the DANGER signs and other cars and holes. He saw me and said, "They're movin' in on us, aren't they?" meaning the East Bay Mud. I said yes sir. His face was exactly halfway between Before and After.

He got out and the ambulance by this time had parked over in front of the orange Thunderbird, which made me think suddenly of Norman and I looked up and there he was, sitting crouched in the ivy by their NO TRES-PASSING signs, Crazy Norman, who had probably seen everything while we weren't noticing. He was sitting there like a statue. He was smiling. Dexter once wouldn't go get his football when it rolled under Norman's T-Bird, and it was easy to get, and I asked him why he didn't, and he said, "Because Norman and my family are enemies—he came over here and shouted at my mother and called her names." I decided that was why she gave us Neighborly Warning. And now there was Norman in the ivy, smiling.

Mr. Mitchell talked with the ambulance driver. Then it was all over. Mr. Mitchell went inside his house and the ambulance backed into Norman's driveway and it drove out where East Bay Mud hadn't reached. I looked at Norman and he looked at me, because we were the only people left. I was afraid he was going to change into a werewolf, but I didn't go back into the house, which would have been a sign of weakness, so I fooled around on the parkway, and then turned on the watering (which was ridiculous because it was the wettest autumn in 84 years in the Bay Area, and it rained out one game of the World Series. I pretended I was practicing, and walked on my hands, but I quit because East Bay Mud had thrown a lot of tar and pebbles onto the sidewalk and it hurt my hands. I pretended to play with the rigs. Finally Norman went away to torture Cheyenne, and I won that round.

I was late for Dylan, but not too late, because I could run it in 10 minutes flat. I decided to wait, and test myself. In the back yard the herd of Dobermans in the other lot were upset about something and began to go crazy. The woman must have cursed them out, or maybe they smelled sickness in the air. I lay on the hood of the biggest rig, and the engine was still warm. The sun was not, though, because it was going fast, so I decided to go get Dylan. I crossed myself like Catholics do when they come to home plate, in case Norman was still spying on me, and I got up. Dexter had escaped from Mrs. Festinger. He was stamping along in the street in his cowboy boots, stamping real hard. He saw me. He didn't know what to do. Words got confused at the front of his mouth and then he said, "When is the Monster going to come out?" It was all he could think of at that point.

I said Dad was at the studio on Thursdays. I also said I was on my way to pick up Dylan at the Kinder Haus, and did he want to come along with me? He always likes to do that especially when Dad and I go down in the gold Dodge Swinger because he likes to play with the seat belt to make the warning buzzer go on and off. Dexter brightened up and said, "I'll go ask my mom—" and then he looked at his house and started to say something else, and then he just ran down by the lemon tree into our back yard and those goddamn Dobermans started up again, going crazy.

So I thought Mrs. Mitchell's Big Crash was a closed case. But it wasn't. That very same night I was upstairs in Dad's bedroom, watching him do the commercials on Thriller. I had fast-talked him into taking our new Zenith Chromacolor Portable up there because I said Mrs. Sampson likes to read her church stuff downstairs, which is true, and the living room is the only comfortable place to read, which is also true, and that I wanted to watch "The Waltons" from 8 to 9, which is true again. The thing I did not say was that I wanted to watch Thriller after Mrs. Sampson fell asleep, which I could do in peace with the earphones. In case she checks on me, I put a dummy in my bed, pillows—she can't see, her eyes are so bad she couldn't even get a driver's license. So there I was royally set up in Dad's bed, and I don't know if there was a siren or not, because I had on those earphones, but right in the middle of *The Bride of Frankenstein* (Dad was doing the breaks in his Countess of Titicaca costume) there was this funny red light flitting around on the walls of the master bedroom, which scared me shitless, and made

44

me think I was going crazy. It took me about 30 seconds to realize I wasn't crazy and the red light going around the walls was real. It wasn't all in my mind. It was coming from outside, from another pale blue ambulance from Highland Hospital, stopped in the middle of the street in front of the Mitchell house, just like before except this was midnight.

I turned off the Zenith, put on my slippers and robe, and crept downstairs and there was Mrs. Sampson, black and asleep again. I sneaked across the yard, which was still wet, and crouched down right in the middle of the Secret Passage, which is that hole in the hedge, and I could see everything. One Highland Hospital man was running out and saying, "I got to have that pump!" and he got it and ran back inside. I kept waiting there, crouched. And then they came out and she was in the stretcher this time, and they put her into the Cadillac ambulance and pulled out. At the corner of Buena Vista they turned on the siren. Then, right behind them, here comes Mr. Mitchell, pumping along in a raincoat, and he gets into the cream-colored beat-up Plymouth, and he roars away after them, his tires squealing. That was that. Two crashes in one day. I got out of my hiding place in the Secret Passage and walked carefully over there in the dark.

Dexter was in his p.j.s in the open door. I said to him, "What happened?"

He was in shock, he couldn't talk.

I said to him, "Come on over to our house, and we'll watch TV."

He turned around and ran and bounced off a big old chair and just kept going.

I walked in, not really knowing what I was supposed to do, and I just looked around and found myself in the kitchen. There was a glass of tea on the kitchen table, so I smelled it, and it wasn't tea. It was booze of some kind.

I went upstairs, where I had been once before, and looked into his mother's room, where the East Bay Mud man gave mouth to mouth, but the square yard of pills had been cleaned up. It smelled all musty and the sheets and blankets were dragged all across the floor. I went down to the front room again, and I called out, "Come on, Dexter, let's watch TV at my house," and there was the same no answer.

I probably should have done something, but I didn't. I'm not about to go ring doorbells, with a tale of misery that isn't even mine, that's the Festinger Department. I figured Dexter was safe, anyway, and so I just peeled home.

Which is where I realized my problem. Old Jack The Bear was in his goddamn robe, with no keys, and on his way to investigate he had closed the door behind him. I was, as the old saying goes, locked out. Up shit creek without a paddle. 86'ed. Wiped out.

I could, of course, just ring the bell, and Mrs. Sampson would wake up and let me in, but then she would report it to Dad. I could explain everything, but I didn't want to. So I jumped across the porch which runs along beside the french doors, and I could see her, zonked out and dreaming of Jesus and suffer the little children to come unto me, which is her idea of a bedtime story, and I prowled around getting wet from bushes. I made the complete grand tour of our house, and it was all locked. But I could see that up on the second deck the window-door to the bathroom was open, to clean out the smell of a craparooney, and I decided that Dad must have forgotten to close it. I went up the gray stairs and took a flying leap to the Mitchell house, which is jammed up right next to ours, not 3 feet away, where they have miniature balconies on the windows, only 2 people at most could stand there, 3's a crowd. Then I pulled myself up one of the poles where they could hang shower curtains

46

all around their sun deck if they wanted to sun-bathe in the nude in privacy, which maybe years ago they wanted to do, and I listened for Dexter, who was still in there somewhere. The hard part was the gutter for rain, which wouldn't support my weight and broke off while I was hanging on. I fell and the gutter bonged me on the noggin, and I was sure the whole neighborhood would hear. But no. So I cleared my head and just went into the house, because the Mitchell sun-roof door was unlocked, and I even went into her room again, and opened the window and stepped out onto her balcony and I had a clear shot at our roof. I closed her window, and took my life in my hands, and jumped onto our own roof. I walked across it and let myself down onto our sun deck and walked in through the bathroom and I was home free.

I was also wet. I changed my pajamas, and threw the old ones down the chute, bombs away, and got into Dad's bed to watch the concluding episode of *The Bride of Frankenstein.*

I knew right away, when I saw Dexter coming home from school. I was out there on the curb, thinking, and he came along with his lunch pail. He looked like an angel, or like a girl. His face was all soft and rosy and sweet, he looked embarrassed, and he wasn't stamping along bam-bam-bam in his boots, he was just walking, and he said to me, "Do you like my new shirt?"

It was okay, and I said I did.

He said his mother was dead.

He stood there, and I said I was sorry to hear that. He doesn't know about us. When he asked, the first week, I told him Mom was in Europe on a special news assignment.

Now I wanted to tell him the truth, but I still didn't. I said, "I asked you to come over last night and watch TV, but I guess you didn't hear." We weren't looking at each other now, and we both knew. There wasn't any car in front of their house, so nobody was home.

Michael, the black kid down the block, came up to us, and he said to me, "Did Dexter tell you about his mom?"

I said yes, and offered them the old apple juice. Michael said he'd take chocolate milk, as usual, Dad gives it to him all the time, and so we stood around in the kitchen.

Dexter said his new shirt was one that his mother was saving for his birthday, on October 28, and now his dad gave it to him early.

Michael said that on "Creature's Features" he had seen plenty of times where people say formulas over the coffin and the dead person comes back to life again. Sometimes they're buried alive and still come back. He was raising false hopes, and I said, "Bullshit." I know enough about false hopes myself.

Dexter said his aunt was coming in from Phoenix, his father's sister. Which I know means it is his grandfather's sister.

I really wanted to kick the shit out of Michael, that whole false-hopes rap, even if he didn't know what he was doing. Teach him a fucking lesson, *never* to. But while I was on the edge of it, thinking I'd throw the chocolate milk in his eyes to confuse him and blind him, as I rumbled on in, which is sheer foolishness, Dad drove up in the Dodge Swinger, and we were all going to go get Dylan at the Kinder Haus. We were standing there around our car when old Mrs. Festinger, the grandmother, pulls up in her ancient Mercedes and gets out and hauls her grocery bags up into her arms and starts up to their house, and she calls out, "Dexter, is your father at home?"

Dexter still looks like an angel. He calls out to her, "No, and neither is my mother because she died last night."

Mrs. Festinger had a little fit, with her grocery bags. She looked at Dad, because he was the only adult present, and Dad said it to her with his eyes, and she finally took her groceries up into that house.

Michael decided he really didn't want to go along for the ride, and went home. So Dad and I and Dexter went to Nursery School. Dex was playing with the seat belt again, and he said, "I guess my father will just have to marry again."

Dad knew I was catching glimpses of him, and he was catching glimpses of me. We didn't talk. Dad said to Dexter, "Is your dad okay?" Dexter said, "I can get out at the next corner," and so Dad knew you weren't supposed to ask. Dad smoothed it over by asking Dexter to roll up his window because Dylan doesn't like to have too much wind in the back seat, and so Dexter stayed with us the whole round trip.

When we came back—Dad at the wheel, Dexter in the front seat, me and Dylan in the back—some neighbors down the street that I only saw once or twice were there on the sidewalk beside the East Bay Mud DANGER signs, and the woman was holding a pot of yellow flowers. She talked with Dad while Dylan and Dexter and I played with cars. Out of the corner of my eye I decided she was going to leave the flowers at the front door, on the WELCOME mat, where you could probably trip over it in the dark and fall flat on your face, especially Mr. Mitchell.

And Mr. Festinger came out for a bow, he had to put in his 2 cents' worth one more time. When Dexter and Dylan were throwing balloons off the porch, Mr. Festinger Earthquake McGoon asked Dad if "the boy next door" was at our house.

He could see clearly that he was, and Dad was irritated by that "boy next door" shit—we know Dexter's name.

Mr. Festinger said, "There has been a tragedy in the family."

Dad said, "We heard."

At this point Dexter came out onto the sidewalk, and

Dylan started to cry, probably because he always says things are "MINE," and Dexter had his red balloon.

Mr. Festinger said, "She's not dead, you know."

Dad said, "What?"

Mr. Festinger with his pork-chop mutton chops, he said, "She's in intensive care."

We didn't know, none of us. Maybe Dexter had been exaggerating all along.

Mr. Festinger said to him, "Come on, Tiger, we got dinner waitin' for you."

Dexter didn't want to. He ran behind the house.

Mr. Festinger went back up to his own house to slap his retarded son in the face again.

Dad looked at me. He was obviously confused. We were all sort of hanging there, getting a chill.

And then Mr. Mitchell came home, and we found out that Mrs. Mitchell was really dead all the time. It was pretty hard for Dad to ask, and so he didn't, but Mr. Mitchell, who was halfway between his two selves, talked about the funeral service. Which was tomorrow, and he invited Dad.

Festinger must be out of his mind, or misinformed. Or something too shitted to think about. Later that night we decided, Dad and I, that he had just heard an early report, and so we can't blame him. But I do.

Norman was across the street at his lookout. I think I'm the only one who noticed. Sometimes when you are in a daze you can take photographs in your own mind, and they develop later.

So we started taking care of Dexter, even more than before. What else could we do, when his father was under what they called heavy sedation, but he'd been under that all the time. For example, we took Dexter along on a rainy day to buy Dylan his new trike. It's a red, white, and blue one. Dexter stole the trike from Dylan and he, Dexter, rode it to the car. Which is another thing I don't get—Dylan is always so happy to see Dexter, and he's always saying, "I want to play with Dexter," when Dexter isn't even nice to him like I am. Sometimes I think Dylan loves Dexter even more than me, he's so happy to see him. My own brother is screwed up.

Dexter is crazy with everybody. Like Dad had another woman over for dinner, she's a secretary and also a receptionist at Channel 2—I guess Dad is running around—and Dexter came in and wanted to know when the Monster was coming out, and Dad said not today, so Dexter walks right up to the woman, Peg, and he pinches her tit. Just like that. She spilled her martini on the couch and Dad sent Dexter home but he stood out front for a while, kicking the front door. Pinched her right in the tit on the nipple part.

We're supposed to forgive him because his mother died. And if anybody in the world should be able to understand what he's going through, it's me. Sometimes when you're lonely you just strike out at the nearest thing. Even old Dylan knows more about things than we think. He'll be playing quietly with his cars and he'll say right out of the blue, "I am a bad boy." And Dad says, "No, you're a good boy." Dylan says, "Nope, I'm a bad boy, but I'm sorry." And when you're in that frame of mind, things just keep happening to you. Like at the Petting Zoo, at Knowland State Park, Dad was snapping us with his Minolta, and Dylan was riding the tortoise and freaking out with the baby elephant, and then a goat ran him down. It wasn't the goat's fault. It's nobody's fault. Things keep happening.

But some things are people's faults. We had a bad scene, for a change of pace, when Dad took me aside and said, "Jacky Bear, I want to talk to you about something."

I saw the shit-storm coming, and I was racking my brain for what I'd done, probably he had started counting his joints and knew I was smoking. It was at night after we'd put Dylan to bed, and I knew Dad had something on his mind because he wasn't looking at me. Now he was, beside the fireplace. He said, "These are pretty hard times and people get confused, sometimes they say things they don't mean."

I was in the dark.

"Jacky Bear, you know that Mom and I had lots of problems, really hard problems, but we loved each other very much, and she always loved you and Dylan as much as I do. And that's total. You know that, don't you?"

I said yes and wondered what he was leading up to.

"And it was never a question of fault, it was nobody's *fault* that Mom and I had to get off by ourselves. And what was tearing us apart was that we both loved our boys so much. K?"

K, I said. I was still in the dark. Dad hadn't blown any dope or got drunk, he was just serious. And I was just sitting there while he went on talking.

"I'm saying this because I don't want *you* to get confused, and tell people that Mom never loved you."

I almost didn't hear it, like I heard it the second time, like an echo in the silence. "I never said that."

"Jacky Bear, your mom loved you *completely*." He paused. "Now Dexter told me today that you said your mom didn't love you, and you didn't miss her."

So that was it. Dexter's out of his mind. I said, "I never said that, *never*."

Dad was looking down at his slippers. He wasn't convinced. He slowly took out a Marlboro and lighted it. "Dexter must have misunderstood. Now we've got it straightened out, okay?"

He didn't say K, the way we always do, he said *O*-K. He believed Dexter, a proven liar who kicks you in the nuts, and pinches nipples.

I'd give anything to take it back, but I said it. "I hate you."

Dad went to the window. "Don't tell me tomorrow that you didn't say *that*."

I went to my room, it was the last straw.

That's why I beat the shit out of Dexter, with my own two fists and no weapon, though it would be very easy to get a knife these days, all the kids at Crocker have them. I waited for Dexter after school and I said, "You gonna pay wif yoah ass," like I was black and bad, and I punched him and scratched him and even kneed him, though not in the balls like he does. Mr. Festinger came out and told me to pick on somebody my own size, which is pretty funny because he kicked me in the butt and he's three times my size. It really hurt for 2 days, he got me on my tailbone.

Later on, when everybody calmed down, Dexter remembered I said that you can't just go on missing your mom, and I tried not to do it, you got to pull yourself together. Which is a completely different thing, and even if I tried to be kind of tough and casual about it I *still* don't see how he could think I said that I didn't miss her. Or that she didn't love me—that's *his* mother, or grandmother. I won't say he's Not Guilty, it's more like a gray area. But I am clearly Guilty, because I beat him up, which solves nothing. Like Dylan says, "I am a bad boy, but I'm sorry." Fuck it, I have enough trouble to deal with. I'm going down fast.

Who isn't? I was feeling so lonely and out-of-touch I wrote a letter to my best friend back in Syracuse, Joe Romano. We were in Scouts together, the Blazing Arrow Patrol, and we used to play tackle football on our knees in the old Playroom, we really creamed each other and rang our chimes, and he saw me with Dad at the circus that time and he said I was a "Natural," and I saw my first cunt in his attic in a magazine that once belonged to his father, who was a POW in Vietnam. I wrote to Joe, including news of some of my troubles, and on the envelope I printed PERSONAL: DO NOT OPEN, so his mom wouldn't read it because she would not approve. A week later I got a phone call from Joe at about 9 P.M., which means it was midnight in Syracuse, and all he could say was, "Man, I am wrecked out of my mind." He's completely messed up and taking heroin—actually shooting smack, the whole needle bit—at his age, 13, my best friend. He didn't make sense except he said he was charging the phone call to Mr. Hudson, who was a prize shithead algebra teacher we both had, but it took him about three minutes just to tell me that, and I had to keep saying "What?" "What?" like I was hard of hearing.

So adults and kids are all fucked up, both. Even Dad, who always follows the comics in the *Chronicle* with me every morning, and now sometimes can't even read them because he coughs so hard. Twice now he's coughed up blood into his hands, and Dylan just says, "Daddy have a cough, it hurt him." Thanks a fucking lot. And Dad goes into trances with those women he sees, and maybe he's lonely and maybe he's horny and maybe he thinks he should get us a substitute mother, but when they are blowing dope downstairs and I hear him say crazy things like "Suddenly in the street, this shattering cold, I am in a bottomless bar and a Viet Vet and my eyes are the jungle and I cannot breathe, where is the America I dreamed of, now on this dark street?"—just *crazy* stuff, it scares me and makes me sick at my stomach, and sometimes the Bay Area women walk out on him because they don't like it either. Who would? He tried it on me once, and I said to him straight out, my heart pounding away, "Don't talk that shit to me because I don't want to hear it," and he looked very scared and lonely, and it did some good because he's stopped. He's stopped with *me*, I mean, but he even does it on the phone, I listened in as usual upstairs, and a woman will tell him to sleep it off, and he'll say that's the trouble, he can't sleep, and it goes on and on and he'll finally calm down and say, "Well, I'm a shmuck," which I am beginning to agree with even though it hurts like hell to say it about your own father, especially when he's Dad.

But everybody's got it, it's running wild like an epidemic. Dexter, for example. I happened to find about 6 of Dylan's toys over there in Dexter's room, even the psychedelic green ball that just looks gray in the daytime but at night gets all spooky and monster green because

57

it has radium like on several watches. We looked everywhere for that, and Dexter had it, along with cars and trucks. I didn't tell on him, I have been shitty enough to Dexter, I just brought the stuff home and carefully put things under beds and couches, and Dad was overjoyed to find them when we vacuumed. I couldn't tell on Dexter, he's so pathetic. Even after I busted his ass, a few days later he offered me a nickel to play with him. One thing I do watch is my words. He has theories about how if he holds his breath until he faints it'll all be a bad dream and she'll be alive like before, but he never can hold it long enough to faint. I've done stuff like that, standing on the roof in the midnight wind and wanting to exchange my life for hers. I also suspect Dexter, that time he cut himself on the hand, of thinking his blood can bring her back from the dead. He keeps showing off his wounds. He also has plans to kill Norman because he called her names. Shit. It's a great neighborhood.

You can never tell what's going to happen next. One night everything seemed to be better, and I was down in the basement with Dad, in his Growlery, and we were talking about our project, which is a Horror Hall Of Fame, to be constructed in Bogeyloosa Louseyanna, with a scholarship program for disadvantaged monsters, and then crash! bam! slam! here comes Dylan down the stairs, headfirst on his red white and blue tricycle, and he flew over the handlebars like he was shot out of a cannon and we had to rush him to the hospital where he had five stitches in his chin. Dad said, "I never thought I'd pick him up alive." He was sure he had fractured his skull. Christ, we were running around crazy, Dad shouting and Dylan screaming and dripping blood and me ready to pass out.

This all has its effect on Dad, of course, and last week he even did his crazy talk on TV so that the whole world will know about it. One of the personalities he does for the commercials on Thriller is The Hippie From 20,000 Fathoms. Last week he did it, only it was for real, and I could tell he was stoned in fact, and not pretending, because of his half-closed eyes and the slow way he talked. He said things that he says anyway, in real life, like about how he makes people nervous and it must be his breath, or his vibes, and when he walks into a crowded room on some enchanted evening all the people edge into protective groups because Man is in the forest, shit like that. He really *does* talk that way, and it's not The Hippie From 20,000 Fathoms or Caesar Asparagus, it's Dad himself. The movie that night was *The Invasion of the Body Snatchers*, another one of my all-time favorites, and then Dad has to open his big mouth before the East Bay Dodge Boys do their pitch, and he says, "Like, man, I don't want to bring you down, but check out what this movie is really saying. It's about Communism, the Red Scare, can you dig it?" So I sat right up in bed, wearing the earphones while black old Mrs. Sampson drowsed-out on the couch downstairs and I was scared because Communism and the Red Scare is something I know all about. Grandfather Glickes, which is Mom's father, was blacklisted because of all that a long time ago in Hollywood where he was a writer for movies, and that's why all my life he has been a bitter man. *The Invasion of the Body Snatchers* is a horror movie about beings from outer space who come into a town in California, Santa Rita, and they are seed pods that grow at night into human beings, and then they replace real people and look just like them so that only loved ones can tell the difference. Like a little kid at the beginning knows his uncle isn't really his uncle, and he can't explain it, he just *knows*. It's one of the pods. All the pods care about is survival, and they're not kind or tender, if a dog gets run over in the street they couldn't care less. They have no human emotions. All they want to do is reproduce and take over the whole world, replacing us all, one by one. It's a nice movie. So Dad, in his costume as The Hippie From 20,000 Fathoms, says, "Like look at the date on this flick, 1956. Do you know the mid-fifties? Don't write it off as a simple case of I'm hot for your pod." He giggled, and I adjusted the flesh tones so it was like an acid trip, I was that mad. He went on, "Check off the points: it is about Godless beings who come into our communities and reproduce cells, got that?—*cells*, and even your neighbor could be one, and they have meetings in private homes to discuss how to take over the world, and you'll see at the end that they export their revolution secretly, and America better wake up to the enemy in its midst, The Enemy Within, and stamp it out. So now you know what's happening here, and if you don't want to think about it, don't think about it, sit back and enjoy." Dad faded out, in psychedelic color, and *The Invasion* came on again, in black and white.

I was too upset to go on watching. When Dad and Mom met each other and fell in love, it was partly because both their parents were Communists, Irish and Jewish, even though nobody proved they carried the cards, which is the way you can tell. I simply could not understand why Dad would even mention it on Thriller. We've had plenty of experiences, like when Dad was refused for the Peace Corps and the FBI man came into our home, with a notebook. That was the time when Mom and Dad said they were going to face this thing together. But that's ancient history, and I don't even know if I would remember it if it wasn't a family story. It's a bad dream. But it always kept coming up. Even here, when the nut in Sacramento put the cyanide capsules in dry salad dressings all over the city, in supermarkets, because he said he was against the Vietnam war, and Dad told me it was a fake and a right-wing plot to discredit the movement. I remembered. Back in Syracuse he told me about his father, and the sweat shop, and getting up at 5 A.M. and working all day until he was ready to drop, which he did when I was pregnant in Mom, his old Irish heart finally gave out, so I never met him. All I know is you're not supposed to turn your back on the workers. I won't. But I'll be a lot more careful than Dad. Sometimes I think he's just asking for it. Mom did, Grandpa Glickes did, it's a family trait. I'm stuck with it. Maybe I wouldn't have beat up Dexter without my Communist background. Dad says we *bristle*. I know I bristle. Like a porcupine. I smell danger and my quills go up, like a reflex. Don't Touch Me, You Fucker. Which is a pretty funny thing to say when you walk on your hands and ride a unicycle.

But there are things you just can't protect yourself against, they just happen. Dylan, for example, driving that red white and blue tricycle down the stairs headfirst. He did another idiot-school thing, when I was supposed to be in charge. I was running the water for his bath, because I was told to give him one, and my kid brother was fooling around in there while I went to get a fresh towel from the linen closet, and he locked the goddamn bathroom door from the inside. I stood there in the twilight and I told him to get his ass in gear and open the door or he'd be in Big Trouble, which he understands (the pillow), and he tried to work it, but he just said, "I can't *do* it," which is the way he does. And that meant the bathtub would overflow, and the water would break through the ceiling down into the living room, and it would be all my fault. I tried to break the door down, but I couldn't, because the house was built in 1921 and it is very well made because people cared about their workmanship back then in an earlier time. I scooted down into the basement and looked for a screwdriver because I thought maybe I could take the lock off, but they didn't have a screwdriver and all I could find was a hammer behind the ping-pong table on the shelf, and I thought maybe I could beat it off, and I tried, but I just creamed the knob. Dylan was crying again, and I could hear the water pouring, but then the light bulb went on in my head and I remembered that Dad always leaves the window open over the sink, for ventilation so it won't stink after you dump your load, and I ran down the hall and out onto the porch and climbed up the place where you could hang an awning, like in the Mitchells' house—I guess all Oakland houses have it—and I made it up onto the roof. Then I got over the open window which you push out, you don't raise it, and it was three and a half stories down to the back yard, I got a little sick looking at all the space and tree branches and there are 3 cables there to the utilities pole, which is P. G. & E., and I could get electrocuted if I missed, but I just took off on a wing and a prayer and made it to the top of the window, which now as I think about it is old and could have broken off and I'd have been killed or injured for life, but I got in, over the sink, and turned off the bathtub water just before it overflowed. Dylan was just standing there, as if he had nothing to do with it, and I wanted to hold his head under water to teach him a lesson, but I didn't. We ought to have a sign in front of our house, BEWARE OF CHILD.

What I did do, to punish him, was take him out back after the bath, after I dried him thoroughly, and I pretended to play with him, but I got the Dobermans all excited in the next yard, and I ran away and left Dylan there all by himself, I even pushed him down next to the fence so that the dogs could bark and howl and gnash their teeth right into his face. I hid in the trees under the porch, so that if a Doberman really escaped I'd be there and kick him in the face and pick up Dylan and rescue him. I didn't want to hurt him, just scare him. I watched him scream his heart out, while I was standing there (heh-heh-heh) and finally I went down and took him in my arms. He had pissed all over his pants. I changed them upstairs, and took care of him. He took a while to calm down.

All of which goes to show that I am about as much of a Supershit as anybody else, if not more. Dylan didn't mean to lock the door. But I rampage him, and I beat up on Dexter, and I say I hate you to my own father. It's pretty discouraging. Dad once said to me, "It's not easy, being an asshole."

Two things I haven't explained. One is my name, or nickname, Jack The Bear. Dad of course is *John*, and I'm John, Jr., as a legal name, but "Jack The Bear" is a jazz record by Duke Ellington. Dad says it's a "classic," and he has the original record and also a tape for his library. I've heard it many times, and it's pretty beautiful, I have to admit, and now when I listen to it I can remember all the fucking bedtime stories Dad used to tell me about the "continuing saga" of Jack The Bear. He really is a kind of legend. And sort of a loser, too, because one of the famous things people always said about him was

> Jack The Bear, Jack The Bear
> Take all them steps
> And get NO-where.

He keeps on truckin', but he stands in place. I know the feeling, especially lately. Still, the music is fine, and when we listen to it together we sort of lie back and close our eyes and smile. I know he smiles because I open one eye to check.

The other thing I haven't explained is my sex life. That's because there isn't all that much to explain. I've never even come close to doing it with a girl, but I have a pretty clear idea of how to. The most I've done was last spring in Syracuse when I took Diane Green to a Saturday matinee at the State Theatre and I put my arm around her shoulder and kissed her, but when I tried to put my tongue in she got up and sat an extra seat away she was so pissed. I lost my confidence. If the truth were known, I behaved like a spoiled brat, I just walked out of the theater and she had to take the bus home alone or call her parents. No wonder she never spoke to me again.

Out here the kids are way ahead of me, physically, and especially the black kids, who mature at an early age. They are amazing. Michael's older sister, Sondra, is only 15, but you'd never know it she is so fucking developed. She has this enormous red Afro. Man, you could hide candy Easter eggs in there and never find them. She was in a black high school drill team in the victory parade for the Amazin A's, and she pretended not to see Dad and Dylan and me on the curb, because of the color thing. Dylan got all excited, and he shouted, "There's Sondra, there's Sondra," pointing at her, but she just glanced over and then looked straight ahead again, out of pride. I heard she had a money-raising project when her folks were away for the weekend, and Sondra auctioned off her clothes in their basement for a whole bunch of guys. I mean obviously that they didn't get to keep the clothes, they just got to see her take them off. I wouldn't pay a dime for a stupid shoe, but I know quite well what I would pay for, and I like to imagine a bunch of us down there in their basement, if they let white guys come, which probably they don't, and I get a wonderful sick feeling in my stomach when I think about it, especially if I'm looking at one of Dad's *Playboys* that he's left lying around. Sometimes in my room I pretend I'm Sondra herself, which is a laugh, but I just enjoy the whole shit out of it, and at the end I dance around the room naked while the crowd cheers.

Sondra comes over to baby-sit on an odd-job basis, when Mrs. Sampson can't, and I pretty much stay to myself because I get tired of her saying, "What you lookin at?"

I really wanted to bring a girl home for dinner, and meet Dad, but I wasn't sure which one. I'm medium popular at Piedmont, but the girl I really wanted, Anita Hendricks, is going steady with a guy who's already in high school and can drive. Loreen Watson is very plump, which turns me on, and I asked her if she could, and she said she'd think about it. So then I went into a waiting period for a week, because I didn't want to rush her, and then finally I did ask her if she had reached a decision, and she had, and it was no. I was crushed, naturally, and I didn't even ask her for reasons. I know she's attracted to me, but it must have been that fucking stupid mistake I made, riding my unicycle to school, people probably thought I was showing off, which I was, and somebody let all the air out of my tire and I had to walk it to the gas station.

Finally I decided to accept my fate, that I would probably never have a date until my college years, if then. I had a vision of a Saturday night in 1979 when everybody in America was out on a date and Jack The Bear was sitting at home reading the *In And Out Book* to Dylan. The way things were going, Dylan himself would probably date before I would, and he'd be nice about it as he trucked on out the front door and I would shed a tear. When it starts bad, I can't seem to do anything right. I was on the edge of a nervous breakdown. Shit, I would have settled for a kind word and a friendly smile.

Which I got, and it's always darkest before dawn, from Karen Morris, the beanpole, who is a head taller than me and works on THE PEST. She liked my poem in the Poet's Corner, which is in the middle of the first page. She said it showed out-front sensitivity. So just like that, without even thinking, I said, Would you like to come to dinner at our house next Friday at 6 o'clock and she said without even thinking Sure. At lunch I went down 3 blocks to a Jack In The Box and called Dad and told him what had happened and was it K? and he said of course K, and maybe he should invite someone so that Karen wouldn't be surrounded by just 3 men. I thought for a minute, and wished Mom could fly back into the world.

But I stopped my mind wandering and I thought about what I had to wear and whether or not Dad would drive me. I definitely decided against his driving, even though Karen said her house was on Cedar Way, which is almost a mile from The Pink Fang.

On the big day when I went to get her, it looked like it might rain, and by now we had gone beyond the wettest year in the Bay Area in 84 years, now it was the wettest since 1849. If we bring luck wherever we go, as Dad says, we also bring rain. I was wearing my Levi hip huggers and my boots and my flowered shirt with a lime T-shirt underneath. Dad thought I should wear a sweater, but it wasn't color-co-ordinated, and so I took a plastic see-through umbrella which didn't clash.

Karen gets her height from her father, who offered me a glass of V-8 juice which I drank with my trembling hands. Karen's mother is totally ordinary, and I was surprised at how exactly she didn't surprise me. Part of the reason I was shaking is that I was afraid they'd ask me about my *family*, and I had already rejected every remark, but they didn't, they only asked about school. I made clever statements as if I didn't care. Karen came down in a green and yellow dress which went well with my flowered shirt, and she must have brushed her hair ten thousand times because it was long flowing dark silk. It was my kind of hair. She was wearing little gold earrings that Dexter would like to steal, they sort of danced and hung around there from her lobes. A little brother or sister watched us through the posts on the stairs, in its pajamas, and we took off. For a block I couldn't think of anything, and my pits were wet, but she solved it by talking about THE PEST again, and that kept us going for three more blocks. It started to sprinkle so I put up the plastic see-through umbrella and we had a hairy old time walking close together, and I looked up at her face and she was slightly sweating too. When the sprinkle stopped I didn't put down the umbrella because it was a good excuse.

Finally at home, Ms. Peg Edinger from Channel 2 had arrived, and she and Dad and Dylan were all at the piano like a family. We eased into things and Peggy, who is very good-looking, hung up Karen's sweater. We made the necessary introductions, and while Dad and Peg had martinis Karen and Dylan and I had Safeway lemonade. Karen talked to them about THE PEST, and praised my poems and stories, which of course pleased me silly. Also, Karen must be the only kid in the Bay Area who hasn't seen Dad on Thriller, but she promised to watch because now she had a very personal interest. To break the tension we turned out the lights and pretended to play the flashlight game for Dylan, but we were really playing it for ourselves, and I hid with Karen in the guest-room closet and squeezed her hand and she squeezed back, I almost kissed her, but then here comes Dylan saying, "Where's Karen? Where's Karen?"

We had goulash, which is Dad's specialty of the house,

and he also let Karen and me have some red wine with water. Karen said she had had plenty of wine before, because the kids usually drink it when they are blowing dope, which really cracked up Peggy Edinger. It was a successful dinner. With candles, and Peggy tossed the salad. Dessert was sherbet, which Dylan calls sherbert.

Dad and Peg changed Dylan while Karen and I put the stuff in the dishwasher, and then Dylan came down for a kiss and went to bed without a peep except for 2 calls for Babar his toy elephant and also a green car. Then the four of us played Crazy 8's and also doubles in ping-pong, the men against the women, and it was no contest. Dad was upstaging me a little bit, which I was thankful for, because he has a skill for smoothing out the hard parts. I hope to be able to do that for my son, when the time comes. The whole evening just zipped along and all at once it was 11 P.M., time to go, and Karen thanked them for a lovely time, and shook hands like a gracious adult. Dad was also pleased with my behavior because I could see it in his eyes and his general attitude. He was amused that I was growing up so fast. They offered to drive us because it was raining, but we said we liked to walk in the rain and this seemed like a good night for it. So Karen wore Peggy's raincoat, which just fit, and I wore mine, and we put up the old plastic umbrella and took off.

"I was being sincere," she said on the street as we went around a puddle where East Bay Mud hadn't helped. She said, "It was really a lovely evening."

"I hope there'll be more," I said, like I was some leading man on TV.

She got thoughtful. Her dad was going to be transferred to San Jose and my heart sank. She said it was a wonderful opportunity for him and she wouldn't want to stand in his way even though it meant losing a lot of old friends.

"And new friends too," I said, and she stopped under the street lamp and we had a kiss, and her mouth was open, not at all like old Diane Green in Syracuse, so I just stuck my tongue in there like a pro. It was a little awkward with her so tall, because she had to stoop, but we did it for maybe a full half minute and then she looked at me and took my hand and we walked hand in hand. Old Karen might even go down for all I knew. I got that sick feeling in my stomach, and that was great because this was really happening, I wasn't making it up, and nobody could ever take the memory away from me.

We sang in the rain, together, "You Are My Sunshine," while we walked, and singing beats talking any day. It's far out, to sing in the rain with the person you like. We were in Seventh Heaven in Oakland. When I get my growth, as I'm waiting to do, we'd make a perfect couple if it weren't for her dad going to San Jose.

When we got to her house on Cedar Way, the lights were all on bright, so that meant her folks were up and we couldn't be alone. We could have stayed outside except for the rain, which was now pouring. She said, "Won't you come in?"

I said, well, I'd like to be with her alone. She knew very well what I meant, and she considered it for a while, and then she said we could sit in her father's car, which was parked two houses up the street because her mother's car was in the driveway, and they had made their garage into a playroom. I said K, and so we went by all the wet cars and it wasn't locked and we got in and sat there, me behind the wheel and the see-through umbrella just sitting there on the sidewalk open. Karen took off Peggy Edinger's coat, and we sighed, it's so lovely and close in a car, and she said, "Don't you want to kiss me?" and I replied by doing it, the old tongue hanging in there again. We kissed maybe for five minutes without a break, breathing through our noses on each other's cheeks, and I was so happy I thought my heart would burst. Then she did this amazing thing, and put my hand on her boob. I pretended to take it in stride and pressed and held it, my very first, and then I explored the other one and she said, "More." That freaked me out so I tried to go down in under the green print dress and her bra was too tight, I was fumbling and making a mess of the whole deal, and she said wait a minute.

I sat there with one arm draped on the wheel, Mr. Confidence Long Hair, and she took off the bra just like that, after she zipped down the back of her dress. She let it fall to her waist and I could see everything, both of them. I said, "Oh, wow."

She smiled, Karen Morris, the beanpole. Her tits weren't that bad, though not completely developed.

I put my face there and kissed her right on the left nipple. I didn't even know where I was, it was that fantastic. She put her hand on my hair and said it was beautiful.

Her other hand started touching me down there, another real surprise, and I'm a little shy about not having anything more than peach fuzz, but I figured I definitely should not blow my first big chance. So I unzipped and let The Monster spring out. She held onto him and pulled, she was kind of growling, and I didn't tell her it hurt. She just yanked away and I sucked one boob after another, there in the rain in the car, and who knows what might have happened if a car hadn't come and we panicked out of our minds and zipped up and crouched down. The headlights were like the police. I knew it was a bust, and when the car went by she said, "We should be more careful."

I said right on, in my mind, and I couldn't get old Monster back in there until he quieted down and was taken limping off the field, though God knows I tried.

One good thing is we didn't feel overly guilty. We got out of her father's car and made a pact for Sunday afternoon. She said she really did want to see me again because I was sweet. She ran her hand through my golden locks again and she was posing like the cameraman had her in focus. I told her I'd be waiting. She's so fucking tall. I was holding Peg Edinger's raincoat.

We went in, and said hi to her folks, and they had no idea what we'd been through. Karen winked at me when she said goodnight. She's a real nut.

I flew home, holding the umbrella and the raincoat, about as happy as I'd ever been in my life. Sex is an adventure. A week from now we'd probably be actually fucking up a storm. We'd fuck all over the place. Just fuck fuck fuck. Our Guardian Angel in the sky would look down and say, Wow, those kids are fuckers. We might even do something crazy.

I calmed myself when I approached the house and did some deep knee bends in the rain. I smelled myself for telltale signs. I peed in the Mitchells' hedge and looked at my own prick, which now had been held and yanked by a chick. I said to him, "Little man, you've had a busy day." I knew I would never be the same again. I just felt confidence, having my own prick in my own pants.

Confidence is what Norman lacks. He had already come over to our house a few times to borrow money, and Dad always gave it to him. But the night after I saw Karen, Norman came over crazy, and he was chewing gum and wild-eyed. He couldn't stop talking. Dad tried to calm him. There had been some kind of minor accident involving the Green Molar garage door, and some shingles were missing and Norman kept looking back there and saying, "Look at that door." He was strange. He said he had no friends.

Dad said, "You've got one friend," and put his hand on Norman's shoulder.

Norman jumped back, sort of jumping forward at the same time, and he said, "You touched me, you put your hands on me."

Dad said, "K, put your hands on me," and he held out his own hand.

Norman couldn't understand for a minute, and then he could, and shook hands. He said, "Give me five dollars and I'll go home."

Dad made a little mistake there, because he said, "I don't want to buy you off."

It was a mistake because Norman took his stand, shaking his head as if Dad had said something repulsive.

I knew Dad was trying to help. But I also knew he had been drinking Bloody Marys, and he's never good after vodka. He said, "Norman, do you have a drug problem?"

Norman just shook his head, disgusted, standing there in his boots.

I could have told Dad, just look into the man's eyes carefully when he's not looking, and you can see that gray old Norman does not have a drug problem. But Dad was being Grand. He was playing Encounter Group and talking to Norman who you do not talk to like that.

Norman smoldered away there in the hallway beside the sunroom and looked back and forth and when Dylan brushed into him on his trike by accident Norman said, partly as a joke, "I am going to whip and beat you," under his breath. I heard it, but Dad did not. Dad was in a world of his own. He felt called upon to do something spectacular again.

I thought to myself Norman Go Away, Norman Just Go Home. Besides, the Manhandler Beef and Barley soup was boiling over and I had to rescue it myself while Dad was loose and careless and sort of floating in the hallway. Norman said, "Thank you, as one white man to another."

Dad scowled and said, "What does that mean?"

Norman said, "You know what it means." He was slightly grossed out, looking at our family, Dylan on his tricycle and me zooming around to rescue soup and Dad sort of wallowing in space. Norman had our number. He said, "I thank you, it won't be wasted." He held up the five-dollar bill as if Dad should smell it.

Dad said, and I couldn't believe my ears, "Any time."

74

When the door was closed, and Dad had gone back to his Bloody Mary, I faced him. I said, "You blew it."

He looked at me, smiling, and stepped out of the way of Dylan barreling in on his trike.

"Don't you *hear* me?" I said.

"Jacky Bear, what's the matter?"

I started to run and then started to stop and then just leaned. I said, "I don't think you should encourage him."

"Now," Dad said, salting around like he was on slow skates, "you have to recognize—"

And I cut him right off, I said, *"Don't!"*

He was bewildered and hurt.

The soup was getting cold.

He grabbed me.

I said, *"Don't!"* again. I made my eyes slits.

He got the message for once. He sagged back and said, "Right," and went into the kitchen and changed to Pabst Blue Ribbon. In spite of what I said to him he was feeling good that Norman had come to him in a time of trouble. He was happy, getting out the soup bowls and thinking I didn't understand, and calling to us, "Soup's on, gentlemen."

I let it pass, but the very next day my position was proved true. Norman tried to gouge out my eyes like squeezing grapes, squish. I personally add up to a total of the third person he has attacked. Dexter and I were throwing around the football in the street, and somebody had stolen the gas cap on our Dodge Swinger. Dad was good, and didn't accuse anyone, but he knew it was Dexter or Norman or Edward or somebody on their way home from school, so he offered a dollar reward, no questions asked, if anybody found it. Nobody did, obviously. Anyway, Norman was sitting in the ivy that afternoon and we have just got to invent a new race for him—he's not white, and he's not black, and he's not oriental, he is, as I have said all along, GRAY. He is the color of fish that died last month, all dismal and washed up, and I would not be surprised if he has cancer of the skin. He is the picture of unhealth. Sitting there gray in the green ivy with his sword cane, and Cheyenne tied up with the blind eye. I came out of our house, The Pink Fang, after calling Karen Morris, who wasn't home, but I left a message and our number with her mother, who said Karen had remarked at breakfast about what a lovely evening it was, and so I wasn't looking for trouble because my spirits were soaring. But Norman told Dexter with his eyes what a penalty it would be to hit the orange '59 T-Bird with the football, and he came down to stand in the driveway, like he was supervising, and the next time Dexter did it Norman said to come. Dexter did, he looked like he was under a spell. He is Norman's servant, and he gives total obedience.

Then Norman looked at me, 30 years old, an adult, with those black eyes of his in that gray face. He said I looked at him too much, and I remembered Sondra with her red Afro, I guess I do look at people too much, because they hypnotize me when I'm thinking about them. Norman asked me if I wanted to keep my eyes.

I said, "That's a stupid question."

And he pressed me down on the driveway, and his thumbs were going in there until all I could see was red stars and spirals and explosions. Dexter was laughing and enjoying it. Norman had his knees on my shoulders and his thumbs in my sockets. I really thought I was going to be blinded for life and never see boobs or Dylan or Dad or the world again, but I bit his arm furiously and got free, although the long fingernail on his little finger scratched my face and I was bleeding.

I was also crying. I said, "You're trying to scare me."

Norman laughed without a sound.

I pretended to be black, which Norman hates, and I said, "Never again. You got that, mothah? Nevah again." I was still having trouble seeing.

Norman smiled his awful power smile. He had an ace in the hole. Last week when I was standing out there in the rain in my white Levis, Cheyenne with only one marble eye and the other one going fast mistook me for a birch tree and pissed on my leg while I was watching something down the block, and I didn't notice it or feel what he'd done until I saw the steam and smelled it. That was a perfect pleasure for Norman, he got a kick out of it. Cheyenne not only dumps on our yard but takes a leak on me personally.

Now Norman lunged toward me with those thumbs and the fingernails like little razor switchblades.

I screamed in surprise and it was so loud that Mr. Festinger, who has been laid off from his job and hangs around the house with his dumbbells, came out of his door like a tank. He stopped it. I was shook up there on the street in the new tar from East Bay Mud, and I said to myself, If Karen Morris could see me now—last night I was Superstud, and now I was behaving like a child. Dexter was completely freaked out. We were all silhouettes. Mr. Festinger, who is making a new career for himself coming out of the house to stop street fights, said to Norman, "So help me, you keep your hands to yourself and your dog on a leash." He was shaking with rage. "Goddamn zombie," he said.

We all went back to our own homes. I had one all-time headache, beating and beating in my brain so that I had fantasies of atoms and molecules in yellow. Thriller could do a documentary on Norman.

I lay in my bed reading *Playboy* and thinking about the beanpole. I got all hot and bothered and so I walked through every room in the house, like a prospector or a spy.

Mr. Festinger is high on my Hall of Fame shit list. He's stood for me and he's stood against me, because he pulled Norman off me and he also pulled me off Dexter, not to mention that kick in my tailbone, but his head isn't together. His slightly retarded son, Edward, has a habit of leaning on our doorbell on Saturday and Sunday just when we got Dylan put down for his nap. Edward also does things like hold a balloon way out over the porch at the railing, and tell Dylan to jump for it, which would mean a broken leg, and Edward says, "I tryin' to strick him." So Dad carefully explains to him in simple language not to ring the doorbell because it will wake up Dylan, and come back later. But Edward stages a sit-in, and Dad lifts him up and closes the door and Edward rings again, and Dad goes out and says, "Really, you have to go home now, I'm sorry," and Edward throws his football straight at Dad's face. Dad *bristles,* and he says, "When you want this football back, send your father for it," and by this time Dexter has drifted over and hears

78

that and says, "Edward, you're in trooouuuble." Dad slams the door and sits on the couch for 5 minutes, rolling the football around in his hands, and I know he's feeling bad because Edward is retarded and the only way he can deal with frustration is to strike back. So finally Dad just goes out and deposits the football in plain sight on the parking strip, and we can hear Dexter and Edward playing way down the street. Then about a half hour later we hear Dexter calling his own father to play catch with him, and we forget all about it until at 4:30, while Dylan is still asleep, Edward comes to the door and leans on the bell again. Dad answers, mad and sad, and Edward says his father told him to come into the house for supper and he wants the football. Dad says that he took it out and put it on the parking strip. Edward is upset and starting to cry, red splotches all over his slightly retarded pie face. So Dad catches sight of Dexter playing soldier up in the tree and questions Dexter, who says he never saw it. Dad says we heard him calling his father to play catch, and Dexter says it was his own ball. He says, up in the tree, "I saw you take Edward's football into your house." So now nobody believes anybody. Maybe the person who stole our gas cap from the Dodge Swinger also stole the football, because they were both taken from about the same place, there at the curb. So they're talking loud, and now Edward is blubbering, and here comes Mr. Festinger in a blue sweat suit, and he comes real close to Dad and puts out his hand, to shake, and he whispers, "Don't press too hard on the issue of the football. I've got it. I'm trying to teach this young man of mine to put away his toys, and I'm going to worry him for 48 hours." Dad says that the young man will think that *he*, Dad, is the one who took it. Mr. Festinger says, "I'll assure him that you don't have it." Dad is thinking that Dexter will also think he's a liar, and he looks at me, and all around, and that ends the ridiculous case of the missing football. The game we play most of the time around here is Everybody Lose.

Another example is after Mr. Festinger took Edward home. The lady who's come to help Mr. Mitchell pick up the pieces walked slowly over to where we were all sitting, and she had a big carton of baby food. She told Dexter to go home and wash up and then she gave Dad the carton and said maybe our little one could use it. Dad said thank you, even though Dylan hasn't eaten that junk for at least a year. The woman stood there and said that she really didn't like being here in Oakland, and her sister-in-law hadn't been much of a housekeeper, because the mess was unbelievable, and Dexter just runs wild, all of which Dad and I already knew. She said that Mr. and Mrs. Mitchell—"Tom" and "Etta"—were as close as two people can be, and now he was simply lost. She was a very sad woman, with blurred blue eyes and white hair. She tried to keep a stiff upper lip, but she couldn't, and she went back to their house. I waited, and I said to Dad that the baby food must be years and years old, because Dexter's seven, and Dad said it wasn't for Dexter, it was for Mrs. Mitchell, who had trouble with solids. I said, "What are we going to do with it?" and he said we'd keep it on reserve for Halloween, if we ran out of candy. We smiled about that.

Halloween was the next Tuesday, and it was a real event because it was the first time Dylan wore a costume and the first time I didn't. That's all I'd need, to go up to Karen Morris' house in a bunny suit and say, "Trick or treat." So we concentrated on giving Dylan a real thrill, we let him choose his flame-resistant costume, which was a clown, and we hollowed out a pumpkin and put a candle in it, and put up paper skeletons and witches, and of course Dad put on a costume because he always gets such a kick out of it, and he didn't have to be at the studio until ten for the Halloween Special, so he was really just making up early. We took turns leading Dylan up and down the street, and letting him go up to porches for stuff, which he really enjoyed, and then we inspected the candy for poison and razor blades and ground-up glass and only kept the stuff that was individually wrapped. The single trick that was played on us happened when I was on Guard Duty and Dad was bathing Dylan. The bell rang and I went to answer it with the plate of candy, and there was a fire on our front porch, a wad of newspapers flaming up. I shouted, "FIRE, DAD, FIRE!" And he came barreling like a bat out of hell down the stairs in his make-up and he went out and stamped it out like you do except that what we didn't know was that it was a gift package of shit on fire, somebody had wrapped a couple of big turds in it, and Dad had fallen for the bait, and now he had shit on his slippers. We heard kids giggling across the street in a hiding place.

About sixty came by the house, in all colors and costumes. Right at the beginning a guy about six feet tall with long hair and freaked-out eyes rang the bell and said, "Trick or treat, you got any chicken?" He was just a hippie. Dexter had told us he was going to be a Nazi general with a Luger pistol, which Dad frowned upon, but when he came he was in fact just a devil with a plastic pitchfork and his father was standing out there in the background in a raincoat, under sedation, smoking. An interesting visitor was just after that, and I freaked—it was Norman, himself, in an Uncle Sam suit, and he said he was taking this opportunity to collect contributions for Elder McIntyre, who was a former law enforcement officer running for State Assembly. He had a little speech that he had memorized, old Norman, and he tried to sell Dad a paperback book about the Communist menace. Well, I know how Dad stands on *that* one, and Dad said, "No, thanks, Norman." Norman had a staring contest with Dad for a minute and then just turned on his heel and walked away in his blue coat and red and white pants and his top hat. Dad said he should have given him a Tootsie Pop right where it hurts. There were also 4 kids from the Deaf and Dumb School who had "Trick or Treat" written on little cards with the name of the school underneath.

After Dylan was in bed I called Karen Morris to wish her a Happy Halloween, but her mother said she had gone to a party, which made me feel just terrific. I might as well have at least got some candy out of the evening. I sat brooding about it and I beat up in my mind the guy she was showing her boobs to because I was convinced now that she showed her boobs anywhere, they were a dime a dozen. She'll probably be in *Playboy* in a few years, Beanpole of the Month.

But the real meaning of Halloween, and all the terrible things that came later, wasn't clear until the morning after. Dad was dead to the world, because the Special was an all-nighter, and Dylan was exhausted from all his Trick or Treating, so I was the only one up and around at breakfast. I went out front to get the *Chronicle,* and there was Cheyenne beside the hedge, where he usually makes his dump. At first I thought he was asleep, and I shouted to wake him up and get the hell out of our yard, but the dog didn't move. He was right beside the rear fender of our Dodge Swinger, and the sun was out for a change. I picked up the *Chronicle,* and gave him a friendly pat on the butt, and Cheyenne didn't move. Then I looked very closely and held his head up and it fell back down, plop, and I knew Cheyenne was dead. I couldn't see that he'd been run over or hurt in any way, because there were no guts or blood or tire marks on his fur, but there was something ugly and messy at his mouth like black puke, and the one blind eye was about as nasty and hopeless and in some other world as a dog's eye can get.

I panicked, because I knew Norman would blame us and take a terrible revenge, which he certainly did, to put it mildly. I thought of dragging the dog onto somebody else's yard, which if I had it to do over again I would absolutely do without question, because then the whole thing might never have happened. But there in the morning I saw what a big dog Cheyenne was and I figured I'd make a mess, or the body would when I dragged it, and if somebody else came out to get their *Chronicle* how would I explain? So I went inside and poured myself a shot of Jim Beam and sat by the furnace outlet in the living room because it wasn't a cold day but I was all of a sudden feeling very cold. I sat there for a full hour, trying to figure something out, getting a little drunk, until Dylan started calling upstairs in the front bedroom. When I went up, and told him to be quiet because Dad was still sleeping, I pulled up his shade and looked out the window. It was now almost 9 o'clock and Norman was out there, he'd found Cheyenne, and he was standing erect with his back to the house, like he'd been carved there and was a statue in our front lawn. I pulled down the shade again as fast as I could.

The Vet said poison. Cheyenne had eaten a hunk of meat that had deadly poison on it. I, of course, thought immediately of Mr. Festinger, who had said out loud—he even shouted it—that he would kill that dog. He of course denied it, he denied it to Dad's face. I know for sure that Dad himself didn't do it, because he simply wouldn't and also because he said to Norman on our porch, "Look, I don't poison dogs." But Cheyenne had finally crashed on our yard, wherever he got the poison in the first place, and so Norman had made up his crazy mind that we had done it. He even suspected me, because I had a motive— that time Cheyenne pissed on my white pants in the rain. But I don't even know what poison looks like except that it's supposed to have a skull and crossbones on the bottle. Norman said, not so much to Dad or me but to the whole house itself, The Pink Fang, "You will pay for this." That scared us, and made us uneasy, and Dad went over to talk to Norman's old parents, who are retired, and I guess they halfway believed Dad, but they're spooky too and you never see them except when they pass the windows at night.

Word got around the neighborhood and we were prime suspects because we were new, and everybody else had put up with Cheyenne and his dumps for years. Norman is capable of anything, and I decided he'd probably go after our Dodge Swinger with a hammer at the very least. One thing he did was report it to the authorities, and a man in plain clothes actually came to our house on Thursday morning. He was apologetic because the police had told him about Norman being reported before, they know where he stands. Dad explained very carefully, and it was obvious that the man believed his story. I started to say that I had heard Mr. Festinger threaten to do it, but I thought that would be cowardly and I didn't have any proof. I did say that Cheyenne was half blind because Norman himself had put out one eye by throwing rocks. Dylan added important evidence, he said, "Norman very crazy."

So then things quieted down for a few days and I didn't know how bad it was, because we had decided that Norman was All Words. Then I just happened to be looking out the sunroom window on Sunday while Dad was taking a nap and Dylan was playing with Michael and Dexter and Edward on the sidewalk in front of the Mitchell house. Mr. Mitchell has a big aluminum prehistoric camper always parked out there, behind his beat-up Plymouth, and lots of times kids sit on the back part of the camper where there's a place to put your foot on and also to sit on, if you want to shoot the shit and relax. Dylan knows he is never to go out onto the street, for fear of being in danger of Big Trouble, like a spanking from Dad or a pillow treatment from me, and he was sitting on the camper, which is technically in the street but his feet weren't touching. I saw Norman sitting over there in the ivy, and the kids were playing "Red

Rover, Red Rover, Send Shitface Right Over," etc., and
Norman was looking down the street, and he said, "Send
Dylan right over," and Dylan didn't want to come,
and so Dexter hauled him down and tried to push him
out into the street, just at the point that a brown Oldsmobile came hauling ass right along there from down
the hill, and the driver would have no way of knowing
kids were playing behind the camper, especially with
the afternoon sun in his eyes, and Dylan would have
been a dead duck with his brains splashed out and running in the gutter if he hadn't been Joe Fumblefuck and
fallen down right there where Dexter pushed him. I ran
out of the house like a shot and picked him up and
cleaned the East Bay Mud tar from his clothes and took
him into the house while he kept on screaming. "Want
to play with Dexter," he said, which shows his grasp of
the situation, and woke Dad up. Maybe I just imagine
things, so I didn't tell Dad. But I think Norman was
planning things. He's capable of it. He had timed it perfectly, with the Oldsmobile, and maybe he even had
Dexter under his power because Dexter was the one who
pushed, just at the right moment.

Everything was going wrong. At school Karen Morris was friendly, but I got the feeling I'd never see those old boobs again. She said she was too young to tie herself to one person. Which is something I can hear her mother telling her. In her room, mother to daughter. Barf City. I was sitting in THE PEST room on Thursday lunch, going into my lonely little fella act, and she came in and saw me being forlorn and asked me what was troubling me. I said, "You know." She said, "Do I?" And I smiled my worlds-of-wisdom bull-shit little smile. She said, "Poor baby," old Karen Beanpole Morris, and patted me on the head. I reached up and grabbed a boob, and she let it sit there, my hand, and she didn't do anything drastic. She did a hell of a lot worse, because she said, "Who turned your motor on?" What a shitty thing to say to somebody who is hanging on for dear life. Well, nothing will come of nothing, in Dad's words. It hurts to love someone more than they love you, and it is also infuriating. You're lonely and pissed at the same time, which explains why you can't do the simplest things right. I thought it would make a far-out PEST editorial, changing the names, but people would know anyway, and I didn't want to drag her reputation through the mud, even though everybody else does that shit all the time. I don't even know if she's a virgin, but she must be, but who knows what's going down in Oakland even after three months living in the heart of it. They can always surprise you. There are things I don't even begin to know. Some of the kids probably ball in the park on the way home, or even during lunch hour for all I know. Even Dylan can raise one, I've seen it, a sturdy little dong, and if he fools with himself by accident it gets to be there, and when my imagination runs away with me I see him in the Nap Room at Kinder Haus, banging away some black 3-year-old before Show and Tell. I'm sick. If any responsible adult knew what I think about I'd be tarred and feathered and dropped on an island to live out my days where I wouldn't infect normal people. I can see me out there making dumb grunts at the sunset.

Once you get into that scene, you can't pull yourself out alone. That's why I reached for Karen's boob. Misery loves company and so I even smiled when Sondra down the street was arrested for ripping off the Dime and Dollar store. I had fantasies of police coming with their red lights flashing and leading her down those steps in handcuffs with her notebook over her face and the carrot-colored Afro showing all around the notebook like a fringe, but I just heard about it from a black kid I don't even know down the block while he was playing kick-goal with Michael and I was a Golden Retriever, which means I had to crawl under cars and get the ball in a position of weakness. But old Sondra the Super Fly Chick was in juvie. I could have gone down and posted bail if I knew how and then she could sell me her clothes at a discount for gratitude. I guess I blow things up in my mind. You can't blow up stolen gas caps or turds in newspapers on Halloween, so it's easier to do it with somebody else, and I wouldn't even want to think about Cheyenne getting poisoned, much less make a big mindfuck thing out of it. I prefer just to sit out there on Saturdays on the curb waiting for our Chinese Hippie Mailman with the pony tail who says to me, "Stay Rough—It'll Come," and pats his bag. I'm not even waiting for anything special in the mail, but he probably thinks I am because I sit out there, probably thinks I sent away for a Rocket-Ring from Rice fucking Krispies.

Even Dad and I are growing apart. I don't know how that happened, but we don't have all that much to say to each other these days. I just don't trust him the way I used to. It's not his fault, he didn't do anything, it's just different. I can't put my finger on a single thing. But time seems to be moving a thousand times faster than usual, and everything in the world is so *bright,* like with grass. Dad feels it too. He's pale and his jaw is set. He grinds his teeth when he takes a nap. I made a cross over him three times, to drive away the evil spirits, and he smoothed out a little, but something's still in there like an infection.

Mom would help handle it, if only she were still with us. I've started to brood about her again, and have the dreams, and stare at the photographs. In spite of everything that happened, they loved each other, Mom and Dad, and they loved me completely and Dylan—who was an accident, but of course I will *never* tell him. Each one was for the other the weak spot. He said things, during the separation, when I asked him about it, like "We have a fatal weakness for each other's fatal weakness." Which says it all. But Jesus H. Christ they could fight. And go storming out of the house saying, "You are just impossible," or "I don't have to listen to that," or "I can't stand you another minute." It was grim. I remember thinking that I'd have to choose between them, and it really racked me up. Either way was all wrong. I'm not trying to be fair or anything, like one dumb ass on THE PEST who said in his SportReport that "both teams played championship ball," when it was obviously false, it wasn't even close. That's not my bag and not in my character. But now it's all over anyway, and I just suddenly stop in a room because I've remembered one more time when I was cruel to her. I can be a really vicious bastard. When I was 9, she had a surprise birthday party for me, and I came singin' in the door at noon and there were all the guys at the table, and I was embarrassed because they had heard me singin' and Mom was standing there, proud and happy. I ran crying upstairs, and when she came to comfort me I screamed a lot of unbelievable angry things at her. That's the kind of son I was.

And I remember the times I was sick and she took care of me and called me her bubeleh. Just the other day for no reason at all, I happened to remember the time before we went to Maine and she folded my clothes and put them in the suitcase. I don't know why I remembered that. I just had a vision and she was folding my clothes up, and we were going to Maine again. And then I remembered Dad after the accident, folding up her clothes, and the few things he could not bear to part with, and the things he gave to Grandma and Grandpa Glickes, like that beautiful scarf from Switzerland. Oh, Jesus, every once in a while I write a letter to her, which makes no sense, but I do it anyway. Like progress reports. How could she ever have had that fear of not being loved? Whatever terrible things Dad and I said, or did, she must have seen that light shining in our eyes. She just must have. But we never really knew the pain she was in. One night near the end, when I was there with her and Dad was off at the apartment, she took me in her arms and she said, "Oh, Jacky, you probably don't remember it, but one day when you were only 7 or 8 years old you came bustling into the house, and you said, 'Gee, Mom, isn't it great just to be alive?'"

I don't remember saying it. But I'll always remember her telling me I said it. And she said, "Jacky, how I wish you could always say that."

Me too, Mom. I wish I could.

That Thursday I was on Guard Duty again and I picked up Dylan at Kinder Haus at 5 P.M. and his pants were sopping when we finally made it Home. I think the people in charge could be a little more careful before they send him out into the world with me. I didn't even think about Toddler Pampers, which I only put on him once in an emergency situation, and so I just hauled out another pair of underpants and another pair of pants. No safety-pin trip for me. All I need is to stick him and have him die of blood poisoning, or loss of blood. But while I was changing him in his room and looking around for clean things I noticed a shadow against the shade and I thought it was my always active imagination, so I flipped it up to show myself that it was all in my mind, but it wasn't, it was Norman. He was on the Mitchells' roof, a hop, skip, and a leap from us. He smiled, his power-situation smile, because I'd caught him red-handed. But it reminded me of the scene in the movie *The Thing* when the brave guy kicks open the door to prove nothing's there, in the greenhouse, and it *is* there, like Norman. He is into Pure Evil, based on his mistake that anybody in our house could have poisoned poor old Cheyenne. Like why not let the dog die anyway, in its own sweet time, it's not worth the trouble. Besides being blind in one eye, Cheyenne had arthritis in one leg. I even wonder how he was able to lift it, to pee on me. That dog had nothing to live for. But Norman was so close there, and he so quickly was a shadow against the shade and then just himself in living color (gray) that I got upset. Obviously I should have called the cops. I could have got him for Prowling. But I didn't. I took Dylan down into the living room, and we played with his hand puppets, and it was semi-fun but mainly pretty boring, it was part of my contract on my allowance, and I would rather have been hand-puppet-playing with Karen Morris' boobs, and then he wanted to SLIDE, a big game of his that he picked up watching the World Series, and I have to say, "Go for it!" and he nods his head, he's cute, and he stands there foolishly with a grin on his face, he'll never steal second that way, and then suddenly he goes laughing and falls on his butt and skids twelve inches on the dining-room floor. We did it a few times, and I was getting *very* bored, leafing through the latest *Playboy*, and wishing like hell he could go outside and leave me alone to Take Care of Business (TCB), and Dexter rang the doorbell.

I was up like a shot and said, "Groovy, you take care of Dylan for a few minutes and don't let him go out into the street, K?" I said I'd give him a nickel. Dexter said K. So we settled that and I went up there into Dad's Master Bedroom to coax my dude and think of Sondra in handcuffs and nothing else. Just a minute or two! But I didn't take full responsibility for my little brother, I was too interested in Number One. I also played Sondra, a winning combination. I was dancing naked when the doorbell rang.

I shouted, "Wait a minute," and stood there telling my Monster to calm down. Finally I got him into my jockey shorts and I went down to take the message. I was hot and bothered as usual. The wallpaper was strange, like something new, and I saw original patterns in the green and gold print. The wall was really beautiful. The painting at the landing was crooked, so I stopped and made measurements, and took care of that item. I tapped with my index finger. I was regaining my confidence, I don't know why, probably because I am so emotional.

It was Dexter again. He said, "Dylan's gone."

I was still the Dudley Studly of my dreams. I asked him, "What do you mean?"

"He's *gone*."

I swaggered on out there and said in a matter-of-fact way, "Oh, he can't be very far," but I was worried because he wasn't anywhere in sight.

I looked at Dexter and Dexter was a new person. I knew him when he was just a *boy,* and I saw him that afternoon when he looked like an *angel,* all sort of beautiful and soft, but now he was just weird. I said, "Where is he?"

Dexter said, "He was there," and he pointed to the middle of the street.

"Dexter," I said, "Dylan doesn't go out into the street."

Dexter's eyes were going all wide and crazy, like he was being goosed, and he said, "That's the last time I saw him."

"Come on, man," I said, "this is serious. Don't play games."

He said, "I'm *not*."

I kept on looking at him. I was worried. I said, "Look, man, my brother is my responsibility. Now where the hell is he?"

94

Dexter couldn't talk.

I said to him, very quietly, "Do you want a knuckle sandwich or do you wanta tell me?"

He backed off to his purple hula hoop which Dad had rescued from the rainstorm and propped against the Mitchell camper; it was bent beyond repair. "Dexter, I'm getting tired of you and your stalling, now you tell me," I said, and I clenched my fists in front of me to make my point clear.

He got frantic and said in a whisper, "Norman."

I said, "What do you mean?"

"Norman."

I didn't believe that, because I could see in plain sight Norman's old orange T-Bird parked there as always, and Norman couldn't take him anywhere on foot, because Norman has a limp and Dylan wouldn't stand for it. I could catch them before they had gone 50 yards. "Tell me, Dexter, *now*," I said, and I was 110 per cent Monster.

He tried to run away and I tackled him, it was easy, and I held him there with my knees on his shoulders, and I asked him if he wanted to die. I said, "TALK!"

Dexter was crying and all hurt, he was in pain.

"Norman," he said, "he took him in the car."

"Norman's car is right there," I said, "I'm not blind, and that car doesn't even have a motor."

"Another car," Dexter said, "a white car."

I looked around for some kind of white car, which was ridiculous because if it existed it wouldn't be there.

"Get off me," Dexter said.

"K," I said, "I'll get off if you swear you won't run away."

"Swear," he said, and I got off, and he ran away.

I chased him, but he's a quick little bastard and he slammed the door of his house in my face, and I stood there kicking it and ringing the doorbell, which is what he does to ours. I shouted out at him to let me in. He didn't answer.

I went back and shouted for Dylan not to hide, because sometimes he does that lately and drives both Dad and me frantic, we have to be furiously screaming before he'll call, "I'm hiding."

But he wasn't, not on Thursday at 5:45, when I was the schmuck on Guard Duty and responsible. I screamed for my brother. Then I went back and screamed again, kicking and ringing the doorbell. Then I sat down to wait, which I did for fifteen minutes. I was hoping Norman just took him for a joy ride to scare him, and would bring him back. I even went to the corner, in case Norman let him off there, which Norman might very well do, and I called there too. A lady was in her yard, gardening, and I tried to be casual, I just called, "Dylan, time to come home for dinner." And I asked her if she had seen a little kid who looked something like me, about 3.

She said hello young man, what's your name. She was deaf or retarded. She went back to her gardening, and I looked and looked everywhere, casting spells so he would magically reappear, but our street suddenly was about the saddest and emptiest street in the world, like after an atomic attack. Everything was there, like cars, but all the people had died of radiation in their bedrooms.

I was ready to throw up by now, and I went into our sunroom and called the studio. They said Dad was out for dinner, and could I leave a message. I knew that that meant he would be home in five or ten minutes, but he wasn't, I watched the clock, and every car that went by I ran outside to see if it was Norman or Dad. Finally I made a decision to call O, which Dad had told me to do if ever there was trouble of any kind and now there certainly was so I did. I told the Operator I wanted to talk to the police, and she asked me where we lived, and I told her, and she said where's that, and I told her it was near Lake Merritt, so she put me through.

When the cop answered, I said, "I can't find my little brother, and the kid next door said the man across the street took him away in a car. So I want help."

The cop wanted to speak to my mother or father, but I explained that I was the only person home, and he took down the address and said a car would be right there. I went outside to wait for it, and Dexter saw me and ran back into his house. Before the cops came, Dexter's father did, in that old Plymouth, and he asked me how I was doing. I told him I thought Norman had kidnapped my brother, and Dexter saw it but he wouldn't come out of the house.

It was tattling, but I had no choice. One thing was all-important. Mr. Mitchell went in and then came out pulling Dexter by the arm. Mr. Mitchell hit him hard on the bottom, and Dexter was crying. Mr. Mitchell said, "Tell me, boy, or I'll whale you."

Dexter couldn't handle it, and he said, "Norman did it, I saw him, he made Dylan get into the car right *there*," and he pointed to the street.

"Where did Norman get a car? What kind of car?" said Mr. Mitchell.

"I don't *know*," Dexter said, all crying.

I said, "Dylan would not get into Norman's car."

Dexter said, "Norman *threw* him in, and he locked the door, I saw it, I saw it." He was hysterical. And his father, Mr. Mitchell, was ready to keel over.

Then the cops came up, without their red light on, but fast, and Mr. Mitchell told them the whole story. One of them was fat and the other had white hair. They were listening to Mr. Mitchell like they didn't quite believe him, because he had stopped off on the way home and had liquor on his breath. But he was pointing to me, and our house, and up at Norman's house, and saying things like "That crazy bastard should be locked up," and he told them about Norman assaulting people.

I was living in a dream, a nightmare, by this time. There seemed to be about double the ordinary space between people and things. Somebody dropped the bomb.

The white-haired cop asked me where Dad was, and I said he was on his way home and should show up any minute, I said I already called the studio. Mr. Mitchell was holding Dexter so hard that he was crying, sort of half lifted off the ground by the arm.

The police went up to Norman's house to check it out, and nobody was home. The fat policeman came down their steps quickly and he looked at his white-haired partner, and then I made my move, and explained about Cheyenne. That could be a motive. He wanted to hurt us, though I didn't know why he would pick on Dylan, he should have picked on Dad or me or somebody his own size. Mr. Mitchell said again that Norman belonged in an institution, where he had already been. I never saw Mr. Mitchell so excited, even more than when his wife died. He told Dexter to go inside and shut up, which Dexter did, although he watched from the front window.

When they questioned him, Dexter didn't know what kind of car or whether it was old or new and he had no idea of the number of the license plate, all of which I would have noticed if I hadn't been up there playing with myself and Sondra with her red Afro in my imagination.

One cop radioed in to headquarters, like they do on TV, and I stood by the car in the whole empty world of our street where the wind was blowing a little. The other cop was getting more of the same from Mr. Mitchell. And I wondered where Dad was.

He finally showed up, in the gold Dodge Swinger, and he parked in the entrance to the driveway behind the cops. We all told him at once, the cops and Mr. Mitchell and me with my eyes and then the old body warmth, because I needed to hold him. I was completely fucked up by now and ready to pass out. So was he when he heard, and he leaned on the hardtop roof, and he was still dressed in his TV suit with some make-up on the neck where he hadn't been careful. He fell apart, across the car roof, and then he was hugging me, sort of bent over, but complete, he couldn't bear it. He was blind-sided.

I had an idea that Norman would just swing up the street with Dylan, maybe even with an ice cream cone or something, and then we could all go home and forget about it until another day. But that never happens. Those thoughts belong in a dream world. I was cold, because the wind was worse, as if that made the difference, and while they talked I went inside and upstairs to get my sweater. I told myself it was a nightmare out of my own imagination. In the bathroom in the mirror I prayed to Mom. I went into Dylan's room, which like everything else now had so much space between objects, it was a monster movie or science fiction. But it was real life, and I made his bed, taking out the wood monkey and some of the cars and fluffing up the pillow. I gave old Casper The Friendly Ghost, his punching bag, a K-O wallop. Then I hugged it when it bounced back and said a prayer, even though I don't believe in God or an afterlife. I slammed Casper again, and then I glided through the rooms, and the hall, and downstairs, the kitchen and the dining area and the sunroom and the living room, and I looked outside at the men talking, and then when Dad and the cops started back into the house I shot upstairs as if I were guilty and afraid to show my face. Which I was. I failed. I let Norman take Dylan. I was careless when it was a matter of life and death. I hid in the bathroom and looked at the window where that time I made a death-defying leap, when Dylan locked the door while the bath was running. And sicked the Dobermans on him, while I watched at a safe distance.

In my mind I saw Dad coming into the basement where I was hanging by my neck on a rope over the ping-pong table, and he would say, "Oh, *NO!*" Slowly he'd go around my body and hug my shoes and he'd leave it to somebody else to cut me down.

By 8 P.M. we decided that Dylan was definitely kidnapped, and everybody believed Dexter's version of the story. It was official. Poor Dexter, he was the only eyewitness, and that's all they had to go on. A lot of police came in now, and Dad had changed his clothes into his blue Levis and brown Levi shirt. He put on a pot of coffee which he offered to everybody. The people on the street wandered by, like they did when Mrs. Mitchell died, they wanted to watch. I saw them from Dylan's window, as I rocked Casper. Dad probably thought I had failed. At one point I was going to pee, and Dad was going to pee, and we met each other at the door where Dad put up the sign, DO YOUR THING, and I looked at him and he looked at me, we were both so

101

scared and frantic, and he said, "Hurry up." That's all he needed to say, and I did, I didn't even flush, which sometimes we do, to catch two birds with one stone, and then I listened to his torrent, and then he flushed and I was standing there, and he looked at me before he went back downstairs.

Dylan had been gone 4 full hours.

I went into his room and sat on his bed. I thought about the look Dad gave me.

I wished I could take back all the times I gave Dylan the pillow treatment. I sat there on his plaid blanket, and I vowed that he would show up in a white car, or an antique car parade like the Amazin A's who won the Series, we bring luck to wherever we go, that's us. It was all dark now, his bedtime, and I sat there as I had never done before, and the bed was empty. I listened to the voices downstairs. If I could get hold of Norman with my bare hands, I said to myself, and that's a lie. I know I wouldn't stand a chance. Dylan's probably dead already, all because of stupid Cheyenne who we didn't even poison. It's all a fucking goddamn mistake. I held my breath like Dexter does, hoping to pass out, but I couldn't make it either. You cannot bring back your loved ones from the dead, no matter how much you want to or try with all your might. I know.

I went downstairs a few times. They were talking about Dad making a plea on Thriller, and looking through the photo album for a shot of Dylan they could show. They finally got Norman's parents and I didn't hear that because it was their house. I almost went over, to hide and maybe listen at an open window, but I didn't. Norman had already caused them enough pain, and I guess they had no ideas on this one. But I heard Dad talking with the cops, and it turns out that Norman knocked up a chick two years ago, which must have been pretty weird, and the baby was put up for adoption, and Norman's parents never met her, even when she wrote them for money, and now she lived in a cabin in the forest near Muir Woods. The police investigated, and I took the phone off the hook upstairs and heard the report. Norman had been there. Dylan was alive.

I held my breath.

Dylan was alive, the woman had seen him. It was a Ford, she thought, white—like Dexter said—and they were going out there to question the woman. Cops work fast, you have to hand it to them. With my active imagination I was just content to know that Dylan wasn't cut up and left to die in the rest room of some drive-in movie.

I went back into his room and touched everything lightly with my palms, not my fingers, and I said in whispers, "You are going to be all right." I also vowed never again to give him a pillow treatment.

Dad knew Mrs. Sampson was out of the question for that night, and so he asked Peggy Edinger to come over and be with me while he made his plea over TV. She was cool, and didn't ask me to go to bed or anything, and we sat together at 11 o'clock and watched him on the screen, very pale, and the camera got real close to him, and he said Norman should let Dylan go, just let him go, and there would be no questions asked. Dad hadn't washed his hair, which he needs to do every day or it looks bad. Dad was like he's never been on television, he was nervous and tripping over words. And then they showed the photo of Dylan, the one Dad took downstairs where Dylan was playing on the floor with his cars and Dad said, "Look, Dylan," and he did and it was a great shot, his eyes all bright and wide and a grin on his face. I remember the very night Dad took that shot.

Peggy sighed, and we turned off the set and then sat there for a while together in the Master Bedroom. I was thinking that if we could only get Dylan back and then Dad could marry Peggy, the world would be bright. But we wouldn't get Dylan back, and then I remembered Mom and Dad's fights and I didn't want to live through that again. He knew she was insecure, and he'd try not to notice, but she had a way of sticking the needles in—to him, never to me—and then he'd blow sky high, and she'd say, "Don't, John, please don't," and he'd say, "Oh, *you* don't," and I could hear the name-calling, and then she'd get her strength back and really go after him, and then he'd go, and they just so fucking hurt each other all the time, every day. And then he was "unfaithful," and that did it. I couldn't stand another round of that, night after night.

Peggy said, "Has he got any cigarettes in here?"

I said he did, and I ran down to the Growlery and got them, and ran back upstairs and I just must have tried to move too fast, those flights of stairs, because suddenly I got very dizzy and I thought I was going to faint, and then was sick at my stomach and threw up, a streamy puke that landed right in my hands. Thank God I had already dropped the pack of Marlboros. I went into the bathroom and did it again, straight into the toilet.

Peggy heard me cleaning up, and she came to the door, but she didn't look in, and she said, "Call me if you want anything?"

I said K, and held my hands, both of them, under the cold tap. For some reason it helped my stomach to have cold water run on my hands.

In my dream I saw Joe Romano, my old pal in Syracuse, and foolish scenes from grade school, all coming together, but one fact was clear. Dylan was out there somewhere, probably in a speeding white Ford on a freeway or in a motel. Norman could do all sorts of sick games, with hatchets and razors. Dylan's head could be rolling at this very minute. I know Norman has a pure hate thing with us. That's the thing to worry about, because pure hate is capable of anything.

I went downstairs at 6 A.M. and Dad was alone in the sunroom by the telephone. He was lonely and exhausted, wearing his Court Jester slippers that he's had all these years. It was a sad gray light outside, all dim. He looked me in the face, and he said, "No word yet."

I was still half asleep. I said, "Oh." I sat down, without a robe, on the freezing stairs.

He rubbed his nose, in the wicker chair, the green one. He said to me, "Is it six yet?"

He asked because he can't wear a watch any more.

105

We don't know what happened, the watch he's worn for years suddenly makes blisters on his wrist. He's become allergic. Or, as he said once a few weeks ago, "I can't stand time." And he smiled without smiling. He was going to get another watch band, but he kept putting it off.

I went into the kitchen to check the clock. It was 6:09. I came back out and told him.

He had the phone in his hand. "They're early risers."

I knew right away he meant Grandma and Grandpa Glickes. They're the only people he called that. Early risers.

"It might be in the L.A. papers," he said to me. "And I don't want your grandparents to learn about this through the newspapers." He sighed. "Maybe I'll wait until 7."

I watched him. He was completely finished. Dylan is his son. He didn't blame me, except with his eyes, which might be just in my mind, but I saw right there in that gray light just how much he was suffering. Suddenly he seemed like an old man with nothing to live for.

We had a little breakfast, and we went over the front page of the *Chronicle,* which had used that same photograph they had on TV. Dad kind of jumped away from the table, like he was falling, and I shouted, "DADDY!" —and I haven't called Dad that, "Daddy," for years.

He said, "It's okay, it's okay now."

I went to him and put my arms around him.

He said, "Easy on, easy on," and patted me.

Oh Jesus.

We put our cereal bowls in the dishwasher, and stood there, and he had a little shot of brandy. I almost said, "Watch it on that stuff," but it would have been cruel, so instead I said, "Give me a sip."

He looked at me, and then he handed me the glass, his hands shaking like crazy.

I took a sip. It burned and I shook my head. I said, "Thanks."

He finished it.

"Well," he said, "here I go." And he went back into the sunroom and dialed the telephone, and waited.

I couldn't stand it, I guess I'm a coward, because I didn't want to hear, and I scrammed somewhere that I don't even remember, which floor, I just crouched in a corner, and then it was over. He'd told my grandparents. It must have been a really rough thing to do. Like I know he had to call them when Mom, their only child, died. What a terrible bummer to have to call them with another heartbreak. And they were never on his side to begin with.

He said, "They want to come up."

I looked at him.

He said, "What do you think?"

I said, "I don't know. My first instinct is no."

"Mine too," he said.

"I mean," I said, "they're not—I mean, there's nothing to *do*."

He said, "Well, they could take care of you."

I shook my head.

He said, "I told them I'd call the minute we got any news. I told them to wait."

"Good," I said. I looked at him like a ghost. For some reason I said, "I think you did the right thing."

He said, "There's a first." He sighed. He said, "Are you tired?"

"Yep."

"Let's try," he said, and we went upstairs to the Master Bedroom, the two of us in the same bed. He went out like a light. And then I drifted off, and nobody called us for a solid hour.

I could have gone to school, since there was nothing for me to do, but Dad has good intuition as far as I'm concerned, and we discussed it for 30 seconds and he said stay home. It was Friday. Dylan had now been missing for 15 hours. The Oakland *Tribune* had a picture of Norman that they must have got from his parents or somewhere because it didn't even look like him, it was from high school graduation years ago.

One reason I didn't want to go to school, and would have run away if I had had to, was that I didn't want to talk with the kids. What was I supposed to do, write it up for THE PEST? "A kidnap story is developing in the East Bay . . ." No thank you.

Mr. Festinger saw his chance and came over to be on TV because the camera crews were there by this time. I stuck by my guns and knew he was the real poisoner of Cheyenne, and why the hell didn't Norman steal Edward? I didn't say anything, I just stood there and watched Earthquake McGoon posing for the cameras and pretending to be concerned. Dad was also interviewed, and he made another plea, and thanked the authorities who were co-operating and doing everything in their power. They even asked me if I would say something, and a guy put a mike in front of my face, and I blabbed a plea also, to Norman, please bring my brother back, he never did anything to hurt you—they had big floodlights set up in broad daylight. The cameraman was a hippie type, and he reminded me a little of the guy on East Bay Mud that gave mouth to mouth on Mrs. Mitchell, so I stayed close to him. We liked each other, and he let me look through the lens while we were all standing around.

You could see cop cars and mobile units and all that stuff lining the street. I was inside for a few minutes, while everybody was still out there, and the phone rang. I thought about asking Dad to come, but I picked it up myself and a woman's voice said, "We've found your kid, he's in a house on 636 Rose Street in Berkeley, you got that? 636 Rose Street in Berkeley."

I said wait a minute, and then the phone went dead. I jumped up and ran out, and I screamed like an idiot, "They've found him, he's at 636 Rose Street in Berkeley, he's okay," and Dad and the cops and the TV people all went crazy, and the cops called in to the station from their car, and I threw myself at Dad and I repeated the conversation, and even though it was my fault the first time at least now I was the one to bring the good news. I was pissing my pants I was so happy.

But all my hopes turned to dust. There was just an old man at 636 Rose Street in Berkeley who had reported neighborhood kids for dumping garbage on his lawn on Halloween, and it was probably not a woman on the phone but a girl or a young guy whose voice hadn't changed, and they were just taking revenge using us as the excuse. Another bummer. The whole explanation didn't reach us until noon, but the important fact was that Dylan wasn't there, we had that much by 10:30. I should be more careful, and I will. A firing squad would be too good for me, raising false hopes.

In the afternoon, after Dad made me a baloney sandwich, I walked for a couple of miles and saw houses that I had always liked when Dylan was safe. I closed my eyes to pray and create a magic spell and walked blind backward and fell on my ass. He was my responsibility, but who gives a shit about that except me who really doesn't anyway as long as the main fact is that he's out there somewhere and crying and maybe mutilated. EVIL is LIVE spelled backwards, and the monsters are having their fun. Somebody will race by in a speeding car and drop Dylan's body on our porch wrapped in old newspapers. I suddenly found myself on Cedar Way, but I turned back without going past the Morris house. I slowly made my way back, and on Carmichael the Dobermans heard me coming and started going crazy, barking and whining, and I could just go in there and let them have a feast without thinking twice, but I didn't.

For dinner Dad took me along to the Safeway to pick up some hamburger. He was really falling apart now, and he looked as old as the hills. He turned the radio on, and we listened to some rock music for half a block, and then he turned it off. His mind wasn't on his driving, and in the rush-hour traffic on Grand Avenue he waited too long at the light after it turned green and a guy in a green Buick honked and gave him the finger and shouted something we couldn't hear because the windows were rolled up. He had no way of knowing, but I made a New Year's Resolution in November not ever to do that because you don't know what people's troubles are and what they're going through.

When we got home, Grandma and Grandpa Glickes called again, and they really wanted to fly up from Hollywood, but Dad said no again. I didn't think they would help, even though I could understand that they wanted to come, but they're never good in a crisis, especially him. He just gets excited. Maybe just she could come, Grandma, but that would make more problems than it solves since he would resent us not wanting him.

Besides, Peggy Edinger came over, and I was really beginning to like and not resent her. She just helped with the hamburgers, and brought a salad, and put the dishes away, and talked with Dad. I heard her at one point saying, "You shouldn't blame yourself, John"—I was out in the kitchen, and Dad had just let out a big moan. I have to admit I sort of wanted to let out a big moan of my own so that Peggy would come in and tell me I shouldn't blame myself. I waited awhile and came out, and Dad was sitting there on the couch, looking old again. Sadness has a way of making you older—or, in my case, younger, like a child. You go to extremes.

I went upstairs and had a talk with Mom in my imagination, and I told her to hang on, we'd get out of this somehow. I even had a little fantasy that it was good she was dead because she never would be able to stand this. At least she'll never feel pain any more, or unloved.

The worst part is waiting there helpless, with reporters and TV people buzzing around you like flies. Dad felt two ways about that because he couldn't stand it but he also knew that they could be a big help in getting Dylan back if they used the pictures and description of him and of Norman too. When night fell, and we were by ourselves for a few hours I slouched around and with half a heart I kept an eye on Dad and Peggy, to see if they'd fuck at a time like this, but I am a retired spy, I don't want to play games any more.

I had a rough night, and Peggy came in once when she heard me scream, and then it was Saturday and another *Chronicle* to look at, and the phone ringing with progress reports that all added up to one thing—nothing. Just before noon I went for another walk all the way to Lake Merritt. I saw a kid standing alone in the grass by Fairyland, a cute little guy, and I ran up to him but it wasn't Dylan. I must have been overanxious, because I grabbed him and turned him around and he started to cry. He was startled. His mom was on a bench reading a paper-back book, and she came over and gave me hell. I told her who I was, and the boy looked like Dylan from the back, and she listened to me carefully and apologized. We talked for a while, but it was clouding up again so we split. She offered me a ride home, and I thought to myself that's all we'd need, to have me kidnapped too, and then I thought I was a freak-out fool because she was obviously okay, and if you distrust the whole world you're in serious trouble. I said I'd just look around for Dylan a little more and she wished me luck. She rumpled my hair in a kindly way, but she didn't really give a shit, she just wanted to tell her friends and husband about who she met in the park. I could feel it.

It was raining by the time I got home, and I was getting soaked, so I went right up and changed. There had been a new development, they had traced the white Ford to Econo-Car Rentals. It had license plates 183 FGK. The rental woman recognized the photograph of Norman on TV, and so she checked her records and tried the local phone number he gave her, where he could be reached, and it turned out to be a false number. And his credit cards were traced to San Jose and they were all stolen. It's not 100 per cent sure, because maybe it's another thief, but it looks like it's right, unless the Econo-Car Woman is just trying to get on TV like Mr. Festinger. I don't know about some people. Dad got two more of those crazy phone calls, one raising more false hopes and the other saying Dylan was dead, but they were both complete lies. I have decided most people should not be permitted to run around loose.

The FBI was helping out because more than one state might be involved. Norman's parents have a summer place on the Nevada side of Lake Tahoe. So the FBI ran a check on it, but the report said negative, I heard that on the 6 o'clock news. Norman's girl friend was also inter-

113

viewed, and I don't see how anybody could knock up
someone like that. She reminded me of the photographs
in Mom's books about the great depression, when
Grandpa Glickes was a Communist or a fellow traveler at
least. Norman's old girl friend stuck by her first story,
and she said she had no idea the boy was kidnapped, or
she would have tried to stop it, and she didn't want to
report it in the first place because Norman had beat her
up on several occasions before. Now that she knew, she
said she would be glad to help, but she wasn't going to
live in that cabin in Muir Woods any more, for fear of
revenge, she was going to move to another state and try
to get a job. She was wearing dark glasses. It just gave
you the chills to watch her. I think she and Norman should
have stayed together and raised a family, The Munsters.
But she was the last person to see Dylan alive, except of
course for Norman himself, and she said Norman slapped
Dylan when Dylan peed his pants. I thought to myself,
He's up to his old tricks, he always pulls that one, and it
gave me some kind of comfort. She said she didn't have
any baby clothes, and she didn't have an opportunity to
wash what he had on. She said Norman wasn't vicious,
he was just confused. He never told her where he was
going when he left. And then on the TV they stopped
our story, and cut away to a commercial. She obviously
was having trouble talking. I watched that one all by
myself, Dad was downstairs and Peggy Edinger had gone
off on her own.

I went down to join Dad, and we walked around a
little in the living room, and darkness was falling again.
We were just waiting. We played Crazy 8's, cards, between
phone calls. At the beginning when the phone would ring,
we thought to ourselves, They've Found Him, He's Safe,
but now we'd look at the walls without a word, the ringing in our ears, and we were afraid to answer it because
they'd say he was found dead. So we went to the Safeway

again, we were just living day to day, and it was an exact repeat, an Instant Replay, of the night before. Dad asked me what I wanted for dinner and I said I wasn't hungry, and he said maybe we should just have TV chicken dinners, and I said K, and then we had the wreck. I whiplashed a little bit, but I only blacked out for a few seconds. The guy in the other car was a tub of lard, and he used a lot of obscene words and said, "I'll sue you for everything you've got." He was driving a Cadillac and didn't need any money, and Dad just stood there in the rain, looking at his boots, taking it. He didn't have any fight left in him. It seemed to take forever, with a crowd gathering, and people looking at us. Jesus H. Christ, how I hate to be looked at! Finally the cop car came, and they had Dad dead to rights, because he was turning across a double-yellow line into the Safeway parking lot. But then the cops found out who we were, and they let it go by, and even that old tub of lard changed his attitude and apologized, after one cop talked to him. I still believe in cops, in spite of what kids say, they never did anything but be kind to me. In the rain I examined our rumpled fender and the headlight that was still working, you could see the rain falling in front of it and dancing on a small piece of chrome stripping. It wasn't a serious accident, and we could drive our cars away under our own steam.

Beside the Dairy Products in Safeway Dad bent over the cart for a minute, and I thought he was going to fall, and there was nothing I could do about it except come up and say to him, "You K?"

It took a few seconds, but he said, "Yep. K."

At home we sat there at the dining table, with our TV chicken dinners, listening to it pour outside and breaking all Bay Area records since The Gold Rush. We thought of Dylan and Norman out there in it, driving through the rain. They could be all the way to Kansas City or

Vancouver by now. I thought to myself, but did not say, LOVER BY DAY, KILLER BY NIGHT. Now it was night.

I woke up at least 20 times. I had dreams in which he was found, and I'd wake up so happy and then it was just raining in the dark. I really love that little shit, and I couldn't blame him for anything, not locking me out of the bathroom, which now seemed like a trip. I remembered another time in that bathroom, and I was washing him and telling him his hand was a spider and his head was a balloon, and I scrubbed his dick and said, "What's this?" And Dylan laughed and said, "It's my gold car." He had a far-out sense of humor for 3.

But I didn't think I'd ever laugh again in my life, because now I would never forget him, and how if it hadn't been for Jack The Bear he'd be in his room now sleeping peacefully. Or waking up and asking for a drink of water which I would be so happy to give him, any time, anywhere.

When it was light, just barely, I decided to sneak down to the kitchen for a glass of Safeway lemonade, and I was rounding the corner when I felt something like ESP, and I turned and there was Dad in the sunroom, in the wicker chair asleep, with the phone on his lap. His head was back and his mouth was open. He looked so pathetic there, in his robe with nothing underneath except his Court Jester slippers. There was a coffee cup of tea, or brandy, there on the telephone table, long forgotten. Maybe he was trying magic like I do, with the phone on his lap. I tried to be extra quiet in getting the lemonade out of the fridge, but he woke up and came stumbling in, and his perfect blue eyes were all shot and his body bent like he had ruined his back and couldn't straighten up. Every time I saw him lately I said to myself, He can't look worse than this, and I was always wrong.

"Hi, Jacky Bear," he said.

"Hi," I said, "I couldn't sleep."

He leaned against the drainboard. He coughed. He said, "I know, man."

We stood there.

He was trying to think, and he said, "How's the head?"

"Fine," I said. "You can't see anything."

He looked. He said, "There'll be a bruise."

And we just stood there again. How I wanted to call Mom back to life! He needed her. He didn't have anyone but me. And I wasn't so hot. In the cold and the silence I remembered when they used to cuddle up by the fireplace on snowy nights. I even embarrassed them once, when I was just a little guy, and they were nude, and I had come downstairs holding onto my "JACKY" cup with the clown on it. Those were the days. Gone forever.

I went back upstairs and tried to sleep again, and woke up around 7:30 when I heard Dexter out there in the street shouting, "Ooone, twwwooo, threee," and I said into my pillow, Fuck you, Dexter, and went back to sleep. I wanted to sleep forever and ever, and when I woke up like Rip Van Winkle with his long white beard, I wouldn't get up and see all the miracles that had come to pass while I was asleep, I'd just roll over and go on snoring. I could sleep through a nuclear attack. Karen Morris could grow up and marry somebody and have kids and become a grandmother and grow old and die, and I'd just sleep, sleep, sleep. I'd sleep through my own death, don't bother to wake me, all you folks out there in T fucking V land.

I was wide awake. Dad was holding me in his arms. He wasn't shaking me, just firm and making sure I was awake, which I definitely was, because he was saying, "They've got him, Jacky, they've found Dylan and he's pretty sick but he's alive, Dylan is found and he is alive."

I was dazed and afraid it was false hopes. I was afraid it was just another dream.

"Man," Dad said, "he's alive." He still hadn't lost all that soggy look, and his hair was wild, but he was a different man. He was joyful.

I got out and started mechanically getting dressed, even before it hit me and I could know what was going on. But I did, and I said to a shoe, "He's alive."

Dad shouted to the walls of my room, "He's alive!" He said to me, "Hurry, man." He hauled ass back to his own room to finish dressing.

I zipped into yesterday's clothes, and I went into the bathroom and brushed my teeth with Dylan's toothbrush. I could hear him shouting, "Go, Man, Go!"

118

For my part I shouted, "More Bread!"

He ran in and almost knocked me down and hugged me. "You crazy fucker," he said, and then he said, "Excuse me, man." He was hopping around. He said, "O my God, O my God." You couldn't deal with him—like if you got in his way you'd be overwhelmed.

I myself ran into the banister. What's going on here? Can it be true? Jesus H. Christ. And in the car Dad told me, while he was breaking the speed limit in complete recklessness. They found Dylan up in the woods by the Piedmont Reservoir, which means he wasn't even 5 miles from our own house, and even if he wouldn't talk to anybody they knew it was old Dylan. He was suffering from shock and exposure, but he wasn't cut up or dead. We tore down Lakeshore with our tires squealing, and then up onto the freeway and to the Kaiser Hospital, and we parked in the Emergency Entrance and Dad tumbled in with me hauling my little ass after him, and the nurse at the desk was glad to see us, and she said he was in Intensive Care, but he was going to pull through, and Dad kissed her, which surprised hell out of her, and we went up but then we had to wait.

A doctor came and talked to Dad, and he said the condition was "fair," which made our hopes fall. And mine, anyway, fell further on down when we were allowed to see him in that bed with the tubes and needles all stuck into him. We were allowed to kiss him silently. Oh, how I loved that picture of Dad, when he kissed Dylan. I wish I was a photographer. Dylan was pale and bruised and he had a cut beside his eye. The main thing was his breathing, he was breathing okay, that's what I checked when I had my turn.

The doctor took us into a little empty room and Dad and I sat together on an examining table that had paper on the leather, and the doctor said Dylan had been through a real ordeal, and he had gone about 48 hours without food or water. During that period he had eaten a lot of dirt. The doctor, who had brown hair and a great tan and horn-rimmed glasses, said that some of the dirt still remained in his intestinal tract, but now it was being "passed."

The doctor, Dr. Murray, also said Dylan could not have survived another night. He had a severe cold, and he was running a high fever, which I knew when I kissed him, and who wouldn't after at least one night in an all-time record rainstorm? I myself would probably have died of terror, in the woods in the rain, with monsters all around in my mind and the cold and no shoes, my pants already full of pee. But Dr. Murray said that Dylan wasn't dehydrated. In fact he was suffering from an almost complete chemical imbalance.

Dad wanted to know when he would be out of danger.

Dr. Murray said they wanted to keep him there for at least 2 days, for observation. Dylan hadn't said one word since they found him, which was 4 hours ago.

Dad was hugging me, every few minutes. He was so happy.

Dr. Murray said there was somebody we'd like to meet, the man who found him. Dad said lead us to him. So Dr. Murray did. We went down the hospital hall to another office, a fancy one with diplomas on the wall and a huge desk, and there were four men in there, two of them in uniform. Dr. Murray said, "This is Sergeant Wilfred Stivers, an East Bay Regional Park Ranger. He's the one who found your boy."

Dad kissed him, he was on a kissing trip that morning, and Ranger Stivers was a wimpy sort of guy with a crew cut, but he was the man of the hour.

He explained the whole thing, and he was jogging, which he does every day, around the reservoir, and he heard a whimpering sound, and he looked, and he discovered Dylan semiconscious and the lower half of his body submerged in a creek. So Mr. Stivers picked Dylan up and ran into the nearest house and got an ambulance. That was really all.

It was enough.

They talked about the $1,000 reward from Channel 2, and Mr. Stivers shrugged his shoulders, but Dad said you deserve it, and we were all in a great mood. Nothing really counted now, because we all had the thing we wanted, Dylan. I was thinking to myself, Let those fucking mobile units come, who cares? Let 'em come.

They did. We all had to go through it, the lights and the microphones, but it was okay, and I felt like I had recovered from a long fight with the flu. I enjoyed it. It didn't matter to me whatever they did. Dylan was alive. I could hardly believe that something in my life turns out right, the little fart pulled through. I went into the men's room in the hospital corridor, all alone, and I swirled my dude around in the urinal, writing HURRAY.

Dad gave me a buck to have some brunch in the cafeteria. I went in there, and I was recognized, and they said it was on the house, keep my dollar, and so I just tucked it away for a rainy day and had a bacon burger and a strawberry shake. The nurses crowded around me. I was a ham, and if somebody brought in a unicycle I would have ridden it. I was just so fucking happy that I didn't care. Dylan was alive. You can be excused for freaking out when something like that happens to you, once in your life.

But of course it wasn't that simple, because he was

really messed up. He cried out in the night, and he had completely lost his ability to talk. He just mumbled and moaned. He had lots of bruises, from goddamn Norman, and he also had poison oak and scratches and cuts on his legs from where he crawled through the thickets. It said in the *Chronicle* that he was "still held tight in a vise of fear." Who wouldn't, at 3? They called him a "blond, unsmiling child"—and anybody who has seen Dylan hysterical with laughter could appreciate that. He never used to be afraid of anything, but now his lips were sealed and trembling.

Antibiotics killed the fever. He was making "satisfactory progress." The hospital people decided he could come home, where familiar objects might give him security, but they didn't want him to see the place where Norman grabbed him, that might bring back bad memories. Dylan tried to smile at me, and my heart ached, because I could sense what he had been through. I imagined him wandering around in the rain in the forests the Oakland hills, bewildered and getting bruised, and the lightning and the thunder, and giving up hope and lying down there with his fucked-up head to rest on the mud with his legs in the water of the creek swollen by record rains. They tried to make him walk, the doctors, and he hobbled a few steps and then started to topple, and they picked him up and put him back on the bed.

Mr. Stivers, the hero, finally did decide to take the $1,000 check from Channel 2, but he took a few dollars out of it and bought Dylan some cowboy boots, which fit, but they looked a little dumb. A nurse put them on him, and he got his picture taken, but he started to cry, so Dad took them off and told everybody to clear out. It wasn't touch and go, but it wasn't K either. The main point was that Dylan would make a better recovery at home, where we brought him, after the flash bulbs at the ceremony at the hospital front door. The newspapers

123

and TV didn't want us to leave, because we were celebrities.

In spite of quiet and rest, Dylan still wasn't talking. The nights were okay because he slept straight through them now, but he seemed content just to watch "Sesame Street," both in the morning and the afternoon, and I went on my Lake Merritt walks again, this time jumping. I remembered Mom, and "Gee, isn't it great to be alive?" and now I could say it again. I was in a daze of happiness. I mean, Dylan was in trouble, without words, but you have to look on the bright side—shit, he was alive.

And the words are coming back, like "egg" at breakfast, and "apple juice." He knows our names too, including "Peggy," who's here now, and once again I have to admit I dig her. If Dad asks me how I'd feel to have her in our home, I'd say yes. She's all right. I can talk to her. I get good vibes. Like she doesn't show *false* interest, or make a big deal and try to show more than she feels, she just surprises you in the hall with her energy. She'd like to get married. She has her eyes on Dad. K by me. Meanwhile we all take care of Dylan, watching him recover, an inch at a time, word by word.

His eyes had a petrified ice-cube look, all blue and like wood at the same time, cold and far away, and he'd just stare at you and mumble something. Like "Aw, fuck it." He could have picked it up from Dad or me, because we say it, but not in the same way, so he probably got it from Norman. Dylan would throw a toy car into the fireplace and say, "Aw, fuck it," and turn around and look at us and say, "Want a gun—bang, bang, bang," which of course he couldn't have learned from us because we are down on guns of all kinds, I never even had a cap pistol. But Dylan would point his finger at space, and say, "Bang, bang, bang," and we just tried to distract him to something else.

I myself wasn't talking much, I was listening to that and also to other voices. I'd wake up at night because I heard somebody crying, and several times it was Dylan but sometimes it wasn't. It was a lonely old dog somewhere or maybe nothing except my dream. Also I was seeing things, like Norman. Once I was watching TV and saw a glittering green eye outside looking at me and I ran like crazy—Feet, do your stuff, in Dad's words—but it was nothing. Still, I could swear I saw a green metal Evil Eye peering through the bougainvillea and heard a whisper on the wind. It said, "Come out—come out." I even saw Norman in broad daylight on my way to school and it was simply Joe Pedestrian, nobody at all. I could hide in the Secret Passage in the hedge, and see the blue pants leg go by and hallucinate Norman when it was only Bag Hung Low, which is Dad's name for the Chinese Hippie Mailman. There's too much worry lying around loose. I hear monster footsteps and it's my heartbeat in my ear. And I dream even more about Mom now, and I think she's taking me in her arms and asking, "Jacky, are you happy?" And I don't want to lie, but I have to, and I wake up.

Dylan's right—aw, fuck it.

I tried to warm over some enthusiasm for Piedmont Experimental, but after what we'd been through, school seemed even sillier than before. Even THE PEST was a drag—and sure enough, right on time, Karen Morris said she thought the kidnapping case would be a human interest story. I told her I had to TCB (Take Care of Business) and she could MYOB, which is "Mind Your Own Business," except lots of black kids say TCB and nobody in the world ever said MYOB except me. MYOB, Christ, I'm a fool, it blows my mind. But I couldn't get into the old routine at school, it's all a shuck anyway, everybody playing games at lunch, like Hide And Go Smoke or Ring Around The Roachie. They think they're so funny. It's a Mental Institution. Even the teachers turn on, and Donald stands there at the blackboard, which is green, and he's high and trying to teach geometry. Who needs that shit? I'd like to learn something for later life. And I definitely do not need sympathy when I'm not paying attention and just doodling because nobody in his right mind would pay attention to that. They want to educate "the whole child." I suppose it's because America is fucked up, and people don't believe in the system any more, but I'd like to trust somebody not to bull-shit me. I had a hairy old argument with Vincent, because I decided to call him Mr. Buccino, when the school rule is that you're supposed to call teachers by their first names, and he told me I was being defensive, and I wasn't, I was just being pissed. He told me I was afraid to let myself go, and then I just sat there in front of everybody. Vincent came to my chair and took me in his arms for sympathy, which I could not stand, and he said go on let it all out, and I said I'm going to throw up, which I thought would stop him, but he said go ahead, and bluffed me. I said, "I am being unjustly prosecuted," and he laughed in a dirty superior way and said, "You mean unjustly *pers*ecuted," and I wasn't only wrong I had also made a mistake in grammar. He patted me and left me alone, because Dylan had been kidnapped, but I was hurting, man, I was hurting. Just don't form a circle around me and ask me why I'm weird. I'm going into organic dope. I'll be the first kid on my block to blow up the world. I simply don't understand how a person like me, who is really generous, can hate so much. Hate makes you smaller, but I go on doing it. I am The Incredible Shrinking Hater. I'll walk around the desk top in Dad's Growlery, and climb the lamp, and jump from key to key on his typewriter, and do heroic battle with a spider, and disappear into my own atom of fucked-upness. Is there V.D. after death? Shit, there probably is, and I'll be dead three years and then my nose'll fall off, plunk, into the casket. Meanwhile it's raining up there in the world of the living, an all-time Bay Area record. I think this is called self-pity. Well, somebody should pity you, and I'm the only one left. I really better get hold of myself, I never used to be insane.

Welcome to the club. Most people aren't crazy because they don't think about it. They never saw the glittering eye in the bougainvillea and they never felt the hair rising on the back of your neck until your whole body feels like hot water and nutmeg, whatever nutmeg is, and never knowing where to turn. When the world straightens out, call me, I'll be there. It's your serve, I just hit it back. The world is ping and I am pong. Jack The Pong. If you ping right, I'll pong the way I see it, and even give your ping the benefit of the doubt. Just don't say the problem is my pong.

And then to top things off and make life all that much easier, we answered the door when we were just starting to cook dinner, and there they were—Grandma and Grandpa Glickes.

Dad was pretty good about it, and he hugged and kissed Grandma and shook Grandpa's hand, and said, "Well, this is a surprise." Which it certainly was. He had called them, of course, right from the hospital when we knew Dylan was going to pull through, and he told them he thought Peace and Quiet would be the best medicine, but Grandma said, "We *had* to come." And she kissed me and said how I had grown, and then Dylan came peering out from the living room, holding onto his little blue car, and Grandma shrieked, "Darling!" and squatted down and hugged him too tight.

Grandma said, "Do you remember your *Omi?*" Which is what I always used to call her, and Dylan had just started to do the last time we were together.

Dylan nodded his head, eagerly, when he had the room, and maybe he even did remember.

Dad and Grandpa were standing there in the hall. Grandpa was saying that they had debated, and they weren't going to come, but it's only an hour and a half flight, and he wanted it clear they had already checked in at a hotel. And Dad, with his drink, was saying we had a spare room, and Grandma turned around and said no, the hotel was fine, just minutes away, with a beautiful view of Lake Merritt. So we sat there and talked, and Dad got them ginger ale, and Grandma kept pestering Dylan, and rummaged around in her little suitcase and gave him a package, which he opened, and it was a teddy bear, and Grandpa asked me how I was liking school. They do mean well, and love us.

Grandpa never learned how to drive a car because he's always been funny. It's not his fault, he's one of life's victims. Dad says Success has its own momentum and so does failure. With Grandpa it's all been downhill since several years before I was born. He never got on his feet again, after that blacklist thing when he never could work again for the movies—like those black guys could never run in the Olympics again for being disrespectful to America. Grandpa's very short, and looks even shorter because of his back problem, and walks with a stoop. The lines in his face are so deep that they're more like folds—Dad says Grandpa has got a great face, but I myself cannot see why it's so "great." All I know is I'd be tall without his side of the family working against me. He has a musty smell, like clothes that have been stored.

And not to be outdone by Grandma, he had to get up and go to his suitcase and get out a child's workbench for Dylan, with a wood hammer and pegs, and he had a book for me on somebody called Lincoln Steffens. Grandma noticed our piano and went over and played it standing up, for a minute, and she discovered it was out of tune and had two keys missing. I know she supported the family after The Red Scare, mainly through giving piano lessons and recitals, because even though Grandpa published a book after he was blacklisted he only made peanuts, which you can't live on. My earliest memories of them are about her, and when she played the piano so beautifully. I've always distrusted him. When we'd go to the house in Hollywood he never failed to show me the photographs on the hall wall of him with movie stars I never heard of, and the one with the traitor who gave his name to the committee, and he'd say to me, "You know why I don't take down that traitor's picture?—so that it can remind me that some things you don't forgive and forget." It's the last picture on the way to the bathroom, and I have visions of him going in for the morning's dump, not forgiving or forgetting, plop. But who knows what that's all about, and my main complaint is that he interferes—he always made Mom nervous, and he'd bad-mouth Dad. I remember in Syracuse, a horrible scene, when he said Dad had "a fatal flaw in character." And he called him "that clown," as if it were something to be ashamed of, being an all-star clown with the Clyde Beatty Circus. But they love Dylan and me, because Mom was their only child, and so we're their only grandchildren. And the news of the kidnapping must have driven them up the wall, so they came. Grandma went immediately to the kitchen to find her way around, and they commented that the house was really quite spacious, and so on, and at one point Dad and I were alone together in the hall and he rolled his eyes up, the way he does, and I thought to myself, Well, we can get through this.

We had a different dinner from what was planned, and Grandma did everything, and Dad and Grandpa were scoring points off each other, and Grandma made some mistakes upstairs with Dylan, getting used to our arrangement, but half in my heart I was really glad to see them. Dylan really seemed happy, with all that attention, so maybe their visit was a good idea. After he went to bed, they all had to talk downstairs, and I thought they'd be more comfortable and could speak freely if I hauled my ass out of there, so I did, and watched TV in the Master Bedroom. Dad came up once, and said, "How you doin', main man?"

I tried to roll my eyes up, like he did, and we both broke up. He said he was going to call Mrs. Sampson and tell her not to come tonight. And he did. He was balancing a lot of things in his mind, I could tell, and I held onto him a little longer than usual when he took off for the studio. He was kind of amused by the whole thing.

But, after a pleasant day the next day when Grandpa and Grandma and Dad and Dylan and I all took a drive through Piedmont and a walk around the lake, when it all seemed to be going well, Dad hit the bottle again, and that night all hell broke loose. I saw it coming, because he started at noon, and he really wasn't very much in control, and Grandpa and Grandma were *glancing* at each other at dinner, and when Dad was tucking Dylan in bed he sat down grandly beside him and the bed collapsed. The frame broke at the rear and the slats went down and then the whole mattress and springs crashed to the floor. Dad pulled off the mattress and then the springs and he took his Elmer's Glue and hammered the frame together with the slats and then put it all back together again and said, "Let me make one minor adjustment," and he pushed too hard, and the whole thing collapsed again.

Grandma laughed.

She didn't mean anything, she just thought it was funny, which it kind of was, but Dad said, "Goddamn it, don't laugh at me, I'm doing my best."

That hurt Grandma, and she sputtered, sort of talking to herself like she does, and Grandpa stood in the background scowling and shaking his head.

Dylan was very interested and stepped in to where Dad was sweating up a storm and holding the heavy springs and Dad shouted to him, "Don't step there," and

Dylan shrank back and looked at Grandma and said, "Daddy *scare* me." Dad, pouring more sweat, said to Grandma, "For Christ's sakes, you can hold him, at least you can do that," and he looked at her with the look that kills, and Dylan said, "Daddy very angry," and Grandma said, "It's a joke, you can't take it seriously," and Dad said, "It's *not* a joke, and *I* take it seriously," sweating away, and finally the bed collapsed for the third straight time, and Dad decided to put the mattress on the springs on the floor and forget about the fucking frame.

He was just nervous, he didn't like to look like a fool in front of his mother-in-law and his father-in-law. That foolish bed made him look in their eyes like he didn't take care of us. I knew exactly what he was thinking.

Dylan said again, "Daddy angry at me, he scare me," and Dad felt terrible and hugged him, and said, "No, Daddy is angry at the bed." So then Grandpa, who hadn't offered a helping hand, now offered his one comment, "Don't make him frightened of his own bed." Dad shouted, "And you *shut up*," right beside Dylan's ear, and so Dylan cried again. Dad said, "I'm going downstairs. Come on, Jacky." But on the stairs we heard Dylan saying to Grandma, "It's okay, he going downstairs now," which made Dad feel awful again, he just stood there for a minute on the stairs.

I'm a coward, and I just faded away down into the basement, and walked around the ping-pong table, and then went out into the Monster Gardens and hoped it would all pass. I sneaked up, back into the house, and it seemed quiet, and I got a joint out of the bowl in the cupboard and went back downstairs into the basement and smoked it fast, to quiet my nerves. I couldn't believe how Dad just let himself go.

And then I heard the shout, and I stamped out my joint in the dirt area by the ventilator, and went on up, and Dad had spilled his drink on the floor and then got up to get a paper towel to clean it up, and slid on it, and bonged back into the fireplace, where luckily there was no fire at the time, he was just lying there in the ashes and black logs on the completely demolished screen. He got up, with the ashes sort of spraying away from him, in his sooty green V-neck sweater and his orange pants and high-heeled boots, and slid around swaying, and looking for a refill, and found it, because he'd already brought the bottle in onto the top of the piano.

Grandpa said, "I think you've had enough, John."

Dad looked at him in pure fury, trying to focus his eyes, and he caught a glimpse of me, and he came over toward me but I backed out again. He called, "Jacky Bear."

Over my shoulder I said, "I got to do homework now." And going down the stairs, I realized I was a little stoned, and almost tripped, but the world slowly stayed put for my racing feet, and I made it. I tried to think what I could say so that he could just make it up to bed with a little dignity left and sleep it off. After a while I heard the shower, and I knew he was cleaning off the fireplace shit, and sometimes a shower can calm him down. I went back up again, and Grandma and Grandpa were sitting there in the front room like stone. I rejected a few things to say and so I sat down like a stone myself. And we listened to the shower up there. When he's good, Dad is very, very good—but when he's bad he really is the shits.

So you could see the handwriting on the douche-bag, as Dad used to say. Grandma and Grandpa decided that they should have us, Dylan and me, with them in Hollywood for a week. I wasn't there when the deal was made, so I don't know exactly how it happened, but they got Dad to go along with the plan. And he knew himself he needed the rest, just to be alone and maybe not even get out of bed except to go to the studio, completely by himself—unless maybe to be with Peggy Edinger.

Dylan was excited. He said, "Big trip. Up in a sky in a big airplane, K?"

"K," Dad said. And then he said to me, "What do you want?"

I said, "What's best for everybody." And then I said, "K?" too, trying to be sarcastic, but he just missed it and nodded his head. Even if Grandma and Grandpa never said it, I'm sure they felt it, and made Dad feel it—that he was a failure. Especially Grandpa, who has experience. And what they did say had a point: Dylan should see new things and not stay there in The Pink Fang to be re-minded. Whenever I said the word "Norman," which I did once to investigate and once by mistake, Dylan crumpled. There was not, on that topic, any sign of good old Norman. He disappeared from the face of the earth. I often wonder why he never demanded ransom money, but that wasn't his style. He must have felt great, sitting there in some cheap motel wearing his KILLER BY DAY, LOVER BY NIGHT jacket watching the Tonight Show and beating off into one of Dylan's shoes. He probably rationalizes what he did, and thinks he just put a good scare into us, and we'd think twice before poisoning an-other dog, but if the Ranger hadn't come along in the nick of time Dylan would be dead and then Norman would be wanted for murder instead of just kidnapping.

He's so screwed up he'll probably come back someday, acting as if nothing had happened, and start up polishing that old orange '59 T-Bird. I already had a plan if he tried Dylan again. I'd stand my ground and say, "Ha-*ha*, Norman, it was me that poisoned Cheyenne, it was me all the time and I hated him because he pissed on my leg." Then he'd go for me and forget all about Dylan, and I knew I could outrun Norman, with his cane, and by the time I got him a block away I'd double back through yards and grab up Dylan, who would be crying by this time, and then we'd haul ass down to Safeway. I played out the whole plan, step by step, several times.

But now Dylan and I were going for a little vacation, a change of scene, to Hollywood with our grandparents. And Dad was going to rest up, or drink himself to death. He drove us all to the Oakland airport, and I was watch-ing his face, and in the terminal after he parked the car he blacked out for a minute in a black modern chair. Grandma got frightened, and started calling for a doctor, but Dad came around again. It was the tension. And then they called our flight, and Dad hugged his boys, and

136

I just hope we can all be buried together in the same place back in Syracuse with Mom, no matter when we happen to die. It's possible I will die first, because I seriously doubt I'll make it to 21. And Dad next, out of too much non-stop grief. And then Dylan will go to college, and medical school, supporting himself by scholarships, and he'll be a world-famous heart surgeon, transplanting like mad.

Dad stood there at the glass wall of the terminal waving to the plane, but I don't think he could really see us, because I've noticed you can't. You sort of wave, at all the windows. I'll never forget him standing there, so completely lonely and beat. He knew himself that he couldn't take care of us properly any more. It was the wise decision. But I could imagine him going home to that solitary house and playing the flashlight game by himself, very slowly, and standing down there by the ping-pong table in the dark and beating his head on purpose against a post, and then sitting in the twilight in my room, or Dylan's, and staring straight ahead.

Grandma put her hand on my leg. I turned to her. I was at the window, and she was in the middle, and Dylan's seat was empty because he was exploring in the aisle, making friends and enemies, and Grandpa was in the seat behind us. I said, "Well, here we go."

She looked at her hand on my leg and then at the back of the seat in front of her. She said, "You have to take the good with the bad."

I looked at her, and up into the bluish-gray hair, and then into her sad eyes. She was having trouble too. She called to Dylan not to go too far, and he came bouncing back like a yo-yo. He really had perked up, and maybe he'd forget all about the nightmare.

He enjoyed it when we strapped him in his seat belt, and Grandpa came forward to help out, and then we were moving out, taxiing for take-off, and I looked, and Dad was doing that slow, slow wave there. I suddenly felt that I'd been *had,* and that in spite of their love Grandpa and Grandma came up to Oakland to get one thing, us, and now they had got what they wanted, and they'd always been fearful of Dad and once told him to go to a psychiatrist, which made him furious, back in Syracuse, so I wanted to act out my crazy idea and run down the aisle shouting Stop The Plane, Stop The Plane, but it wouldn't have worked. Dad was the loneliest man in the world. And tonight Thriller was going to do *Abbott and Costello Meet Frankenstein,* and Dad does a great imitation of Lou Costello being frightened—"Ch-ch-ch-chiiiiiick!" I knew the movie because I checked *TV Guide,* so I'd know where he was and what he was doing when I went to bed in Hollywood.

We landed once in San Jose, and once in Ontario, and then we were in L.A., with the four little suitcases, 1 for each, and I had been thinking all along that one of those trained dogs would find my lid of grass in my suitcase in my underpants. The very afternoon before Grandma and Grandpa arrived, I had done my farewell act at Piedmont and bought the dope from our friendly playground pusher, and Dad already had a supply of wheat-straw Zig-Zag papers from a head shop in Berkeley. I was glad of that now, because I couldn't survive Grandpa without being a little ripped.

Their house is small and dark inside, and Grandpa smells like it or it smells like him. We went in and opened up the shades, and Dylan got a glass of milk because he was thirsty, and Grandma already had it set up where we'd sleep, which makes me think they had already planned to get us, even before they saw Dad screw up Dylan's bed and later fall in the fireplace. I unpacked, and I smiled to think what they would think if they knew

I was carrying a lid of real live mary-whana in my suitcase. But the room was familiar to me, old times, and it gave me confidence to be there even when the situation was a bummer. I touched things, and looked them over, and tried to remember the earliest summer when Mom and Dad and I—Dylan wasn't even born—had such a good old visit. I checked outside, in the empty garage, and walking along the two brick tracks, I felt a little happy. It was so familiar, and the air smelled the same. Things like that, the smell of the air, they're so small, but they really help. I almost even liked it inside, looking at the pictures in the hallway of the traitor.

After dinner, which was spaghetti and tossed salad and peppermint ice cream, we sat on the porch like old people, bored, rocking in the swing, and I wanted to turn on, because then Grandma and Grandpa can say anything they want to and I'll mind my own stoned business. So I said, "Let me make sure I've unpacked everything," and Grandma said, "You're such an organizer," and I nodded, and went back in there privately and rolled one, and then I said, "I think I'll take a stroll"—I said, "I'm an organizer, and I'm an explorer," and she was too busy concentrating on Dylan to notice—and so I took a hike, and got mellow, but when I returned Dylan was safe in bed and I suddenly panicked in dope and thought God was trying to suck me off the earth, with his gigantic breath, so I held on hard to the arms of the swing, and said, Fuck you, God, which any Communist could appreciate, although I said it only in my mind, and I thought of Dylan in the forest in the thunderstorm eating mud, and I just held on. Grandpa said to me, "Let's have a game of chess."

I said, "Far-out."

He brought out the board and the pieces in the living room. He said, "Are you feeling up to snuff, Jacky?"

I thought. I said, "Far-out."

He said, "Right-on."

Ha-ha. Old Grandpa The Red, hanging in there. Musty, musty. He put the pieces on the board.

I do not like the way he teaches me chess, because when I make a move he'll say, "Now tell me why you did that," and I know I've muffed it. He says life is war, and chess is life in miniature. You never can be too careful. The other guy always has a trick up his sleeve. Be on your guard. And I myself just want to float and not compete.

I was cold. He got me in a fool's mate, and then he had to show me how to do it, the Devil's Crossroads, and I said I'd remember that one. It made Grandpa happy. What he really wants to do is checkmate Dad, who won't play with him.

The evening wore on, coasting downhill out of gas, and Grandma was nervous, and had to keep thinking she heard Dylan stirring, and they talked a little about Mc-Govern and Social Security, and Grandpa was talking into an echo chamber, or it appeared that way to me in my deranged dope-fiend state, the loser at Devil's Crossroads. Grandma got a sense that it wasn't going so well, and so she tried to calm me by showing me all the photographs in the wedding album, and asking me if I remembered, the last time we looked it over. Which only made me think of Mom, and she saw that, and put it right away again, feeling she had made a mistake, and she wanted to say a few words and talk with me about Mom, I could feel it, but she took off her glasses and rubbed her eyes.

Grandpa, right out of the blue, said, "He's never known what he wants out of life."

Meaning Dad, of course, and why did Grandpa have to mumble that, even if Dad did fall on his ass in the fireplace and create a shitty impression. I stood up and said, "I won't stay here if you talk about my dad that way."

141

Grandpa made his eyes wide, like an owl, as if nobody could blame him.

I said, "I won't stand for it." I was hot-stuff. I told him he could stick the Queen up his ass, and any other piece of his own choosing. Then I fled and ran into the wall of the hallway.

That's me, Dudley Do Right.

Grandpa said, "Let's all take it easy."

I said I had to shit. I went into the bathroom, nodding at the traitors in the hall, and rolled myself another joint. I had an awkward thing on the way out, meeting Grandpa, but he doesn't know, and so I hid the stuff and took another one of my famous strolls to cool off, smoked, and cupped the roach in my hand, and said hello to a fat black guy who was watering his lawn with one hand and drinking a can of Coor's with the other. I thought, When I come back they will have found my stash, and face me red-handed with the evidence, and I'll just walk on my hands down the white line. I laughed under the street lamp, smelling that same air again, reliving my childhood visits.

I made it to bed without another bad scene, only knocking over a small lamp in the dark. The rooms are too little and filled up with junk. On my way into fucking dreamland I thought of Grandpa on the breadlines, and the whole Depression story, and I saw men in overcoats in lines, stamping their feet to keep warm. Then I had a fantasy-dream that I was playing chess against Norman, who probably never even heard of it. But then I woke up around 2 o'clock and I was soaking with sweat, especially around the neck of my T-shirt, and I went out to the kitchen to have a glass of milk, and there he was, Grandpa Glickes, just like Dad is there in The Pink Fang. And Grandpa had his own glass of milk. He is just one more in a long line of adults who can't sleep, not to mention kids. He was probably an okay man until the world dumped on his Communist head. He stood up, stooped, and got me a glass of milk too.

He said, "You love your dad, don't you?"

It was so dark all around the one kitchen light, darkness zonking in the windows on all sides. I said, "He's Number One in my book."

I couldn't believe it, but old Grandpa Glickes, who hates Dad, said, "Glad to hear it."

I held onto the glass. It was a hell of a nice thing for him to say. I think Grandpa believes in *family*.

He stared at his own milk.

We were both a little embarrassed.

He rinsed out our glasses.

In the hall I heard him say something, thinking I was still there in the doorway, but it might be too sad, and there are always those things I don't want to hear.

I lay in my bed, and the Hollywood night was warm in the house and I counted backward from 10,000. I wondered what was to become of everybody. I would have smoked another joint, but I fell asleep, fighting it all the way, man, just dragged down by a failing score in Current Events.

Dylan wanted to play the flashlight game the next night, but the only one they had was full of two dead batteries, and besides you can't play the flashlight game without the old star performer, Big Daddy Himself. So we sat there in Hollywood with nothing to do, except marbles for Grandma and Dylan and that fucking chess for me and Grandpa. Dylan finally went to bed at 8:30, and then around 9 I went back to take a leak and I heard something, and I went in and he was standing at the window, and when he saw me he said, "I think I'll go to bed now," all sort of casual. It made me smile. And it made them smile when I told them. It was just so cool the way when he got found out he said, "I think I'll go to bed now." It was the day's best remark.

I had made one interesting friend earlier in the day, a girl named Micki across the street who was mowing the lawn and is about 17 and looks like a Roller Derby Dropout. She showed me her garage, when we oiled the mower, and she offered me a cigarette, and I said I'd rather smoke something else and she said so the hell would I and I pulled one out of my shirt pocket and said, a ha! She said it was good stuff, which it is, and we talked about where I was from and she went into the house and got some almond Hersheys which she had had enough of by the looks of her pimples, and then we sat in the yellow chairs in the sunlight, groovin on the vibes of the great Hollywood outdoors. She was going to Night School at JC and hated it. Someday she'd be a Private Nurse because there's a lot of money in that, in home care, because they leave you a pile when they die. Her big sister was pregnant and divorced and sleeping inside and calling out in her sleep with daymares. Micki smelled of sweat from pushing the mower and she could kill bees with her bare hands—wham! on the rusty white round table, wham! just like that.

After she got Dylan down for the night Grandma wondered what to do with me, and she took me beside her on the couch, while Grandpa was typing up some book in his den, and she tried to tell me about Mom. I've always sympathized with Grandma, but she showed me some old pictures from 30 years ago, and I was getting very jerky and nervous. She had the best intentions, but I had the old secret combination going around in my brain while I nodded. I asked her to play the piano. She did, and we even remembered that pattern for 4 hands we used to do, it flowed through my fingers even if I was a little rusty. I didn't tell her that all alone in The Pink Fang I'd done some practicing on my own. So I really wasn't a "marvel," not like she said. Grandpa came out for a breather, and we did it for him, and he got some pleasure from it. The whole family has always been musical. I even lost my head and wanted to impress them. I told a couple of jokes, and Grandma laughed and he laughed, and she said, "That crazy guy!" We had kind of a warm scene.

And then I was in bed again, after exhaling my joint out the window, and crushing the roach and carrying it in to dump in the toilet while I heard them in their bedroom watching TV. I was thinking about Mom, and about how Dad hated the idea of seeing a psychiatrist, and what I was going to do with the rest of my own fucked-up life. I pretended I was a black kid, and I said to the dark, "Like you got to choose between two diffren things, you goin to be messed up or you going to get it togethah," just a heavy black dude, I always do that. I don't know why. But I decided I was going to go to Europe on my own, the summer when I'm sixteen. I need the experience.

During the night I had a dream of the black chick down the street in Oakland, Sondra, who wore that sweat shirt that had DON'T FIGHT THE FEELING printed on it, and about how she was taken away to juvie court for ripping off Dime and Dollar and supermarkets and probably whole shopping centers. Well, I guess Sondra didn't—fight the feeling, I mean. And then I woke up and wondered why I dreamed about Sondra of all people and I just sat in the moonlight, and remembered Mrs. Mitchell, Dexter's grandmother, when she crashed for the last time and the East Bay Mud man tried to give her mouth to mouth without success, and I thought that Dad could die and rot there in The Pink Fang, smothered in his own blood, in bed or on his back with a concussion in the fireplace, for weeks. Who would know? Mr. Festinger? And I couldn't walk out on Grandpa and Grandma, but I was suddenly really terrified, I could almost hear Dad's voice calling to me, and Mom's mixed in, you don't know what's happening to you at night when the world is asleep.

My attitude was complete the next morning, Sunday, when Dad actually did call, on the phone, at 9 A.M. A funny thing was that Dylan wouldn't talk to him—and I said, "Come say hello to Daddy," and Dylan for some crazy reason of his own refused. I took him into their bathroom and I said, "Now you talk to Dad, or I'll beat the shit out of you." I squeezed his arms until I must have left telltale handprints, like I was Norman, completely cruel, but even though I regretted it, I knew I *had* to get Dylan to speak to Dad, Dad could not have stood it not to hear his voice, so Dylan shot out from the bathroom and ran in and grabbed the phone, and shouted, "HI, DADDY!" in the new outfit Grandma had got for him, and then he dropped the phone on the floor and ran crying to her, which I don't think Dad heard.

He couldn't have, because he said to me everything was going okay there and he had a lot of work and problems at the studio. I said what problems. And he said oh it was nothing, just the usual. But his voice wasn't entirely convincing. There was some kind of special trouble. I looked at Grandpa Glickes, who was bunched up across the room going into his Communist Owl act again in the rocking chair. And Dad said to me in a kind of sign-off voice, "When you walk on your hands, think of me."

That hurt. For some reason that really hurt, and it made my decision final. I knew where my *place* was. It was with Dad, no questions asked.

I signed off myself, and let him say good-by to Grandma, and I took Dylan back into his room. I told him I was sorry, I didn't mean to squeeze his arms, and I gave him 67 plastic cars to play with—5, actually—and then I sat on my bed to figure out how I'd work it.

How I did it was this: first the money, 2 $20 bills from Grandma's wallet in her purse, which I hoped she wouldn't notice right away because she had over a hundred in there, she's the money manager. Then I excused myself from their walk to the park, with Dylan, saying I felt pooped and a little feverish, and I wanted to take an aspirin and lie down. Grandpa, Grandma, and Dylan went walking, and Jack The Bear was alone in the little house in Hollywood, staring at the Traitor in the framed photograph in the hallway. I stayed cool. My voice has been mistaken on the phone for a woman's, which always pissed me off, but now was an advantage. I looked in the yellow pages under Air California, which is what we came down on, and planned my speech thoughtfully, and then dialed them. They said can you hold. I said sure. Then I tried a German New York accent, and pretended I was smoking a cigarette and called out imaginary things like Harold, de vater's boiling in de kitchen, in the middle. I said, "Do you have a flight to Oakland today, it is for my 12 year old son, you have a space, please? The dumbbell said let me check that through our computer. I said, Hurry pleez, it is a last minute chanz. The clerk said yes, and I said, Ho-k, ve will be at the airoport 30 minutes early, that is the rule, yes? You have the name correct, no?"

As I said, I have a record of fooling people on the phone, like calling to report stolen property or burglars, Dad didn't just teach me back flips. I even did it in Syracuse, I was Strubblepeter, the Kraut Kid with the blond Afro who did everything evil in sight. "Zank you wery much," I said to the ticket agent, "ve vill be dere." I really was enjoying it until the ticket agent was strangely silent and said, "Could you please spell the name again?" I listened, and got scared. I had to decide, and I hung up fast.

That's what made me turn to Micki. I went over and she was there, watching Pro-Football alone on the TV, and she said, hi come in, and I said, Look I got a problem, and you can help me. She said sure. I said, I'll give you the rest of my lid if you'll do it. Micki said, What is it? I went into a big thing about how I wanted to be with my dad, but now I was stuck with my grandparents, and all I wanted was to go up to Oakland and see Dad again, and I had the money but I needed her to make the reservation and pretend to be my mom. Micki thought it was groovy, she even liked the idea. We went over our plans, and I told her what to say, and then she called. There was a bad moment when they asked her to give a local number—and she put her hand over the receiver and asked me, and I said make one up, so she did, and then she hung up and said, "It's all taken care of." I said great, and I'd get her the dope. She said forget it. I said, "No, I want you to have it"—because I was thinking that if she changed her mind that might stop her from telling. So I ran over and got it and gave it to her. She put it

149

behind The Great Books Series and said, "See you in the movies."

I said, "What?"

She said, "Take care of yourself."

I said, "Don't tell, K?"

She got a little pissed. She said, "I've run away myself a few times."

That eased my conscience, and I went out again, leaving her to the Jets and the Patriots. Don't worry, Dad, I'm a-comin'. Though my head is bendin' low. Hold on, the cavalry is on its way.

I decided on Yellow Cab, because I'd seen a lot of them and they seemed friendly. I shot out down to the corner and read the number on a house in the middle of the next block. Then I called, and said come immediately, and then I threw my clothes into my plaid bag, which has my name on it and still the old Syracuse address on a tag, and then I sat quietly at Grandpa's writing desk. I had a long green pencil, and I wrote on his yellow pad, very carefully:

> Dear Grandpa and Grandma,
>   Don't panic. I'm fine. I'll call you later this evening.
> I love you both.
>
>> Your grandson,
> >
> > Jack
>
> P.S. The missing money is my fault, and will be repaid of course.

Then I hauled my ass out of that house, all I needed was to meet them coming back from the park, and I was in a cold sweat because when I rounded the corner the Yellow Cab had already arrived and the driver was pissed off and looking around on the sidewalk with his door open. He made me show him my money. All the way to the airport I tried to think of something, and tried "Nice day today," but he just kept his eyes glued to the freeway, he probably hated long-hair smart-ass kids, and if he knew I was a runaway he would have pulled into a police station and said, "Last stop, buddy, here's where you get off." The whole way I was afraid he'd do it.

I tipped him a whole dollar, not to arouse suspicion, and then there I was in the heart of Amerika, with a *k*, the L. A. International Airport, panting and fucked up, and knowing I'd get caught sooner or later, it was so obvious. But I can stay rough if I have to, and so I bravely picked up my plaid bag and walked into the Air California area—I told the driver to take me to United, in case we were tailed, or they'd investigate later, I was thinking of everything.

And then I sat in the Departures. My plan was to rush to the desk at 10 minutes before take-off, and say Mom was having trouble parking the car, "and please give me my ticket quick, I have the money, you've got my name on the list." I would say my dad was meeting the plane in Oakland.

And I did it, I got away with the whole goddamn rip-off, paying cash, making my face all innocent and scared and pointing to the parking lot, and my suitcase was so small I thought I'd carry it on, ok? and the Mexican guy in the blue uniform said ok, Gate 14, and I flew after I said, "Tell Mom I'll be waiting at the Gate, K?" and he said sure. I was in a big rush, but I stopped because a kid who looked like Dylan was lost in the long moving-sidewalk thing and fucked up, and his mother passed frantic going the other direction, and said "Wait —baby!" and so we played Laurel and Hardy for a minute, and she said, "Thanks," to me and I said, "No problem," and rode it the wrong way again and then the right way and my last hurdle was the Skyjack Prevent metal detector which I passed with flying colors and then there I was seated, cute, admired by the stewardesses, who undoubtedly go down at the drop of a hat, and we had to be cleared for take-off, and the Captain apologized for the slight delay, and then we were airborne.

Send this boy to camp. Or military school, to shape him up and straighten him out. I'll try to be a Real Person once again, and they'll make me run laps around the athletic field with a 500-pound pack, oh, in the sky I wanted to beat off I was so proud of myself making problems for everybody. Beside me was a homeward-bound Vietnamese veteran who sat there drinking scotch and he spilled the first one and said to the air, "Shit, look at that." His hands were shaking worse than mine. And mine shake so bad that if I did want to beat off all I'd have to do is try to hold onto it. Anyway, his name was Vic, he was probably 20 or 21, and he ordered a Bloody Mary at my request and sneaked it to me for a few sips, and if I hadn't given all my grass to Micki I would have given him some because he needed it. He offered me a lift, because he had a Valcar waiting for him, and Lake Merritt was pretty much on his way to his parents' home in Walnut Creek, and I said great. Vic said right away, "Your dad's not meeting you." I froze, but he grinned, and he's pretty studly, with blond very rough bristles around his chin and mouth. He was going to shave in a Chevron station probably before he made his grand entrance to his folks' home, stuff like that floated through my mind. I know cops and soldiers are pigs, but they've all been right on with me. Vic is one of many.

I stood around the revolving baggage claim, with his tickets, and got them off and together while he checked out Valcar. His duffel bag was a ton, I couldn't lift it and had to wait just guarding it. Then we drove on the freeway in a crummy Vega which he hated and cursed, and he pulled off at our exit and said he'd drive me to the door, but I said when we got close, "Just let me off here, I want to surprise the old man."

Vic was chewing gum, and he said, "Take care, good buddy."

Then I waved and he was gone, peeling out in the Vega, and if I ever meet him again, which I won't, I'll say, "Hey, good buddy." He's probably remembering playing touch football at my age, he wants to work for the Parks and Recreation Department, and my guess is he will be out fucking standing. I only hope his girl who wrote him all those letters is waiting there for him, as promised. But as always I doubt it. I am beginning to think I have supernatural powers, because I can always tell when people are going to get shafted and their hopes go down the drain, Roto-Rooter.

I stood there with my lonely little plaid bag on the corner, in sunlight and colder than Hollywood, and then I found The Pink Fang locked. For fifteen minutes I explored and poked and acrobated onto the roof, looking for a loophole, and there wasn't one. Only when I climbed over the garage gate, the one in front of the door itself, moldy decoration, did I discover that the garage-to-kitchen door was unlatched and probably has been for years. I took my plaid bag and went in and sat down. Dad wasn't dead or rotting anywhere, it was just a mess with newspapers and clothes and full ashtrays lying around. I didn't tidy up—I didn't come back for *that*—and I got bored after a while, his stash was gone and the only booze was white wine, which I've never appreciated, and at the window I saw Dexter and Edward playing with that old decrepit blue bicycle, and then I looked at Crazy Norman's orange '59 T-Bird still intact in the exact same spot, like a prehistoric dinosaur, and then I took off an article of clothing in each room, Kilroy Was Here, and ended up in my underpants in Dad's Growlery.

I took the underpants off and ceremoniously put them on the net in the next room, on the ping-pong table, and the doorbell rang, probably some kid for a paper drive at Crocker, and I hid in twilight in the sunroom and then I got out the little red book, dialed Grandpa Glickes in L.A., and he picked up the phone down there and I said, "Hi, I'm okay," sitting there on my bare ass.

He said, "Jacky, is that you? We've been so worried."

I said, "Me too." I'm very sarcastic when I'm naked and freezing my ass off.

"Jacky, where are you?" He was also signaling to Grandma, I could tell, and then her voice all in a rush, "Jacky? Jacky darling?"

My heart ached, because I could tell I had caused them so much worry. I said, "Hi—I'm fine."

"But where are you, darling?"

"I'm fine, just having a little fling, K?"

"But your suitcase is gone, Jacky, and all your clothes."

"Look, I'm *fine*."

"Jacky, we have to know—"

And I slammed down the phone, like the shit I am.

So there I was in The Pink Fang, getting scared about what I had done, and maybe Dad had gone skiing up at Squaw for the weekend, but of course not since he had called that very morning, and was more likely at Peggy Edinger's house. But as it got darker outside and cold in the house I retraced my steps and put on my clothes, and I began to wonder if something might have happened. One night in September he had driven over to Stockton, to Channel 13, TV Diablo, which we can't get on our set, to judge a Tots to Teens Talent Show, and he told me how he was driving the old Dodge Swinger back at 80 mph and suddenly there was a piece of junk in the middle of the road with no lights on and he swerved and fishtailed 200 yards and skidded to a stop and caught his breath and ran back, and the car was pulverized but the Mexican driver was standing there without a mark on him and said, scratching his head, "I don know, she was goin preeety good there." And maybe this time Dad was bombed or something, coming back from Sausalito, and in my mind I saw him flying into oblivion or San Rafael, with the steering column puncturing his lung, or heart, all shafted and drunk or spaced. Well, I am developing a weakness for monster fantasies, it's heredity and environment both.

I leafed through the December *Playboy*, and started taking off my pants again, you'd think it was Back-To-School Week and I was trying on clothes. I was naked once again, and I took the magazine upstairs with me and lay on Dylan's bed, just as I had done before the shit-storm of the kidnapping. I played Ms. Striptease Sondra again, with my famous carrot-colored Afro, fantasying bras and panties whirling off in all directions, and my old pal Rudolph the Red Nosed Mother Fucker rose to the occasion.

Then I was sad, just lying there and thinking. For some reason I remembered when those shits in Syracuse saw my long hair in the McDonald's and said, "Do you think that's a girl or a boy?" and I shouted at them, "I'm a boy —a *beautiful* boy." They didn't appreciate it, but I chalk it up as one of the great replies to a put-down. Then I let my mind wallow around in my most recent adventure, if you're going to run away you might as well take the plane, and I compared it to Tom Sawyer coming back to his own funeral, and that blended into the other book and Huck, and the Duke and the King, all that stuff, and I myself am 100% all-boy, and then I dozed off and reminded myself that I always preferred to have Mom read to me, instead of Dad, because she just did it so that I could turn loose my imagination and get involved in the story and Dad was too flashy and hammed it up on his winning-personality trip. Mom wanted me to like it, and Dad saw it as another chance to perform. I probably could have got some quarters at the airport carrying people's bags. Or by walking on my hands like an accordion player's monkey and doing back flips with my cap lying there upside down, if I had a cap. The best trick, like Tom Sawyer, would be coming back and seeing the Swinger in the driveway and stealthily creeping upstairs where Dad is napping with nightmares and kiss him on the cheek and have him smile in his sleep. Oh, I can kid myself all day long.

There's a whole big wide wonderful world out there just waiting for you, as Dad says with sarcasm. I slept, and when I woke up it was 9 P.M., and I had become a TV star myself, and on the interview the man said to me, "You had training from an early age, didn't you?" and I bashfully nodded toward Dad, who was my business manager now and standing just out of camera range, and I said, "The best." What woke me up was a sneeze, and I sneezed again, because I hadn't put my clothes back on, and I could hear Dad downstairs.

He came to the base of the stairs, and he shouted, "You get the fuck out of this house."

That scared me, and I didn't even think to myself, Well, this is a piss-poor welcome.

He shouted again, "I warn you, I'm calling the police."

I couldn't figure out what the hell he meant. Without even putting my clothes on, I went out to the head of the stairs, and I said, "Hey, *Dad?*"

He saw me and then it was his turn to be completely confused.

"Jacky," he said, like he was going to faint.

I nodded, feeling kind of embarrassed and naked.

He leaned on the table in the hallway, and then he said, "Where are Grandpa and Grandma?"

"Hollywood."

He was in shock. He said, "I don't get it."

I said, "I want to put on my clothes." I went back in there, and I could hear him coming up the stairs. Jesus, it scared me. No more Tom Sawyer shit for me.

"Jacky—oh, man," he said, coming into Dylan's room.

157

I was stumbling into my pants. I sneezed again into my hand, and swabbed it away with a sock, and put it on.

"How long have you been here, man?"

"A few hours," I said. "I took a plane."

"Then your grandparents know you're here?"

"No," I said, and I looked at him like he was a retarded child. Christ, he was supposed to take me in his arms.

"Well, look," he said, "I better call them."

I shrugged my shoulders and sat on the bed because anything I could say could be held against me.

He turned, and started to go, and then he turned back around and looked at me. "You flew up here by yourself?"

My lip was trembling.

"Well, what the hell—" he said, standing there like a seal out of water. He had paint on his Levis, yellow paint, and he'd probably been painting Peggy Edinger's bathroom or something, we painted over there once before. He looked 50-50, not exhausted and not joyful, and he didn't come in bombed, but he was very shook up. And then finally he took a not very subtle hint, and came to me and put his hand on my head, in the back. "So you decided to come visit your old pa." He put his arm around me.

"Easy, man," he said. "I don't know what to say."

And then I was crying.

"Oh, my Jacky Bear," he said.

We stayed there for a while, me sitting and him standing, in Dylan's room, and then he said, "Come on, I've got to call them."

We walked down together, in the darkness. I said, "By the way, I stole 40 bucks from Grandma, to pay for the plane fare."

He patted my shoulder. He said, "If you got any left over, let's go out for a pizza."

I said to him, "Nobody loves a smart ass," which we used to say to each other all the time, and it was K.

But then he sat in the sunroom by the phone, thinking for a minute, and I said to him, "I think I'll go up and shower and shave," and he smiled, and I went into my cop-out routine again, I didn't want to hear the conversation.

But I did, too. I went up and turned on the shower, but I didn't get into it, I ran breathlessly into the Master Bedroom and took the extension off the hook, tripping over a half-full beer can in the dark and making a mess beside the bed, and I listened to it all, and I started to say "Hi, Grandma, I love you," but I didn't, and it looked like I could stay, and Dylan would keep on with them for another week or two, Grandma said he was a light in their life, they had nothing else to do, but she was really fucked up about my running away. She paused and I could hear her thinking, and she was completely freaked out that I had done such a thing.

When she got off, Dad spoke briefly with Grandpa, and I said to Mom in my mind, "There now, I've done it again," meaning I was just guilty for a change, and I knew she'd understand, and then Dad came up and found me in the dark. He said, "The shower's on."

I said, "There's nobody in it."

He said, "Wild." He smiled at me, and then he said, "Let me tell you what we decided and you can vote Yes or No, K?"

"I was listening here," I said, "and I vote K."

"I'm glad." He turned on the light.

Then we could see the beer can turned over and the beer on the floor. I pointed, and said, "You should have warned me."

And he laughed, and he said, "No, man—*you* should have warned *me*."

So here I am in Oakland on Instant Replay. I completely crashed that night—after we had Roundtable pizza and talked it all over. As I went to sleep I wished on a star for old Vic to have something good waiting for him in Walnut Creek, and then I slept for 12 hours. Dad didn't make me wake up the next morning, but I finally did, and when I came downstairs he made us Egg-in-the-hole, which he always gets a kick out of, and I let him think I like it, and then there we were. He said, "You're late for school."

I said, "I'll go early tomorrow."

He grinned, and said, "Eat your Egg-in-the-hole."

I said, "I filled up on the hole."

Every day in every way I'm getting more sarcastic. Dad and I have always done it a little, ever since I can remember, because we are a couple of clowns. And I know that my main goal in life is to have Dad approve of me, even though I don't really approve of him. I'd jump through hoops to please him, and I already have.

"Want to come to the studio?" he said.

"Do you want me to come to the studio?" I said.

"No," he said, "I can't stand the thought of your coming to the studio, but I will make the supreme sacrifice and out of the overwhelming goodness of my heart I will—"

"All right, all right, I'll come," I said.

"No, no, you don't have to—"

"I'm coming, I'm coming—"

"Very well, Jacky, if you must—"

"I don't want to."

"Oh, *please*—"

Et fucking cetera. We are idiotic. And on the way there in the Dodge Swinger with the radio blasting soul music and both of us finger-poppin and dancin in our seats with our seat-belts on, pretending we were K, I thought about Mom, and about Dylan in Hollywood, but there Dad and I were being ridiculous and I felt relieved at the same time as I felt pure sadness.

And on Tuesday I didn't go to school, I put it off again, but Dad made me promise Wednesday for sure. I explored the Monster Gardens of ivy and undergrowth in the back yard, freaking out the Dobermans next door behind us, and I climbed into the noble mossy tree and stared down at the dogs. While they snarled and gnashed their teeth I stood there in the icy tree and looked at the wash next door on the line, it was done by Dexter's father's (grandfather's) sister (great-aunt) who brought us that baby food at Halloween, and is now staying around disgusted and worried and eager to go back to her own home. About seven adult shirts and endless Dexter clothes, and underwear of all sizes, strung out in the sunshine that didn't warm anything up. At noon I went out front and greeted our Chinese mailman, Bag Hung Low, and I took Dad's far-out magazines, we never get great mail. The camper was still parked like a funeral in front of the Mitchell house, with another piece of its aluminum siding ripped off and strung on our hedge. I was at loose ends. The Wandering Jew, which I am by half, and the half that counts since the mother decides what you are. I don't feel like a Jew, but I'll fight to the death anybody who objects to it because I know about the gas ovens and the hatred. Probably Grandpa got pissed on as much for being a Jew as a Red.

And that got me thinking about Grandma and Grandpa, and how Dylan was doing, and I regretted my decision a little.

I stood around out front and Norman's parents drove up and got out of their ancient Chrysler, and I said a cheery hello, but they just looked at me, weird as always, you can see where he got it from. I wasted away the afternoon watching TV and eating a can of Beefaroni, which I ate at 4:30 and spoiled my appetite for dinner. But Dad didn't mind having it late. So everything was really okay at 7:30 that night, except the house was so fucking cold, and I wasn't thinking about anything in particular when I was semi-bored watching "Dragnet" and then something caught my eye at the french doors and it was the glittering eye, a shadow and a point of light in the bougainvillea, and I got very cold immediately all over and said, Stop imagining things, Jack The Bear, and to prove it to myself I bravely walked over to the window-door and then there was a rustling and snapping of branches in the plant and undergrowth and I could see someone running away in the darkness back there in Monster Gardens. I called "DAD!" real loud, and he came tearing down the stairs with shaving cream on half his face, and when I saw him so astonished and spooked I said, "I'm sorry, a cat scared me."

Dad can't deal with it. He's gotten stranger. He's hurting. Like he goes along all smooth and then a big hole sort of opens up and he falls into it and can hardly breathe. We can laugh and joke, of course, but sometimes I come into the room and he's staring into space.

Something is going on that I don't understand and I don't think I want to understand. Like we tried to play the flashlight game Monday night, and ring the little buzzers in the rooms that were put in for the paralyzed lady to signal with. I was hiding under the desk down in his Growlery and he sent a shaft of old flashlight down there, and then I began to make monster noises in my throat, as a joke, and he ran down and grabbed me in his arms and stumbled up the stairs to the living room and turned on all the lights. Trying to catch his breath, he said, "Jacky, my heart is beginning to beat with the monster's heart." He said that. It did not bring me peace of mind. And now he can't even go down to the Growlery, and he is afraid to get TV dinners from the freezer down there, like he is afraid of the dark. He says he hears monsters in the laundry room, whining and whispering and moving around. He didn't mean to confess it to me, he said it all trying to catch his breath to some friend on the telephone, and I just hope it wasn't his boss. But now I can almost hear the monsters myself and shadows beside me make me freeze, I think I'm seeing things and hearing things. It's very heavy. We have to stop. He can go hours at a time, just being his happy-go-lucky old self, but then it hits him, and his face clouds over, and I try to keep up a good conversation but he's only half there.

Dexter was shocked to see that I had returned, and he went white as if he had seen a ghost. He couldn't understand that Dylan was in Hollywood and Dad and I were still here. That's not all he doesn't understand. His older brother and his wife are living there now too, and that must mean they are his aunt and uncle, and they have two very old and beat-up cars, a Falcon and a VW, and you have to push the Falcon to start it, which I helped to do, and Dexter said his so-called brother was 26 and I asked him how old the wife was and he said 2 years younger, and I said so how old was that, and he thought

164

for a long time and said 22. Which in itself isn't so bad, since Dexter's only 8, but he can't even add 7 and 4, he can't subtract 6 from 9—I tested him—he can't do simple arithmetic even when you practically hand him the answer on a silver platter, he just sits there on his bike thinking and thinking and saying, "I'm thinking." Then he says it's not his fault. And he is very bright, or at least normal, so the problem isn't his IQ. I gave him my favorite fortune from a fortune cookie, which I had saved, and asked him to read it, and he could not even read, "Good news is coming your way," which has no hard words. Instead he stared at it, and tried, and got mixed up, and stammered, and then he tore it up. I sent him sprawling and crying on the sidewalk. It'll be years before I get that fortune again, if ever.

Dad and I decided I really should be getting on back to Piedmont Experimental, and I promised, so I did. And I was still a celebrity because they had seen me on TV, and everybody asked about how Dylan was doing, and I said he was on vacation in Hollywood, and they said "*Holly*-wood?" and I said it was no big deal, my grandfather just writes for the movies. Cough, cough. The old beanpole, Karen Morris, descended on me and invited me to a party at her house that Friday night. I said I'd check with Dad and see if I was free, and she said, "I hope so," and flirted with me like she was the half-time show and left me to draw my own conclusions.

Of course I was free, that's a laugh, and I spent all Friday afternoon selecting my wardrobe, and sat in a hot tub for half an hour, and put on Right Guard and Hai Karate and combed my hair for the Dry Look and generally behaved like a schoolgirl going to her first dance. Dad made a sarcastic comment in the upstairs hall and I told him to fuck off under my breath.

I showed up at Karen's house a half hour late, so as not to appear overanxious, and she had decorated their Rumpus Room with streamers and posters and strobe candles, and packed her parents off to a double feature. There was a distinct aroma, along with the incense, and I took a few hits from my good buddy Martin Kwalick. He was flying and he kept saying softly things like "Fish gotta swim, bird gotta fly," and then smiling like he understood the whole universe. Karen came over and said, "Want a fudge?" and I looked all around me, and said "Wow," and she laughed and said, "Men!" She went to change the record, and I said to Martin Kwalick, "Did you catch that?" and he said he could really get into it. We laughed and he passed me the woofer, and I said, "Fish gotta swim, bird gotta fly," and he said, "I was just thinking that myself." Jenny Williams was going by us every once in a while on a skate board, wearing a purple velvet dress and no bra.

I got wrecked, with a little help from Martin, it was incredible stuff, and I devoured 2 Cokes and many cocktail tacos. I was leaning against the furnace, which was hot, and waiting for Jenny to fly by again on her skate board so I could say Here's Looking At You, Kid, like in *Casablanca* which Dad has practically memorized, or just say Hi, if I chickened out, and then I couldn't see her anywhere, not to mention about 7 or 8 people who had been there, now there was only a total of 6 of us in the Rumpus Room. I figured somebody had said, "Let's go out for a pizza," and so I wandered upstairs to the main floor and ate a slice of ham I found in the fridge, and I was just humming and eying a juicy can of Coor's when the toilet flushed nearby and then there was Karen Morris herself striding across the linoleum with glassy eyes and her face all sweaty. Who knows what she was on, but she saw me and came up to me and kissed me when my mouth was full of ham. She said, "Well, come on." I swallowed and followed, wondering what surprise was in store, and she took me upstairs where I found out. She said, "This is the playroom." Actually it was a huge bedroom all dark with a giant water bed and that's where the rest of the party was, everybody giggling and stoned and having a group grope. Karen said, "I found Jack." Somebody on the bed said, "Who's Jack?" And I said, "I'm the one who wants to play doctor." That broke them all up and somebody said, "Climb aboard," which I did gladly, making waves, and Karen did too. Everybody was into the feelies. I stroked a chick's hair that really turned me on until I found out it was Martin Kwalick. Gradually my eyes became accustomed to the darkness and I rubbed my hand under Karen Morris' dress, on her leg, and up and up, while she made the throat noises, and up and up like "I think I can, I think I can," and then I freaked because she wasn't wearing panties and I had a handful of hairy It, my first. She was eating my ear and I plunged right in, the old middle finger, and she started rummaging around at my dude, and unzipped, and there he was again, and she said, "Ummmmmm," and somebody a few couples over was laughing, and I was thinking in my doped state that I'd do it right there, I'd lose my cherry on a water bed in a party commune, which is a lot better than with a whore, as Dad did it when he was 17, he told me in a weak moment when I asked about it, and Karen was banging my monster Freddy Friendly against her leg, and I was hauling myself on top of her when the door opened and the light went on.

Somebody beside me said, "Hey, bag the light," and then an adult man's voice said, "What's going on in here?" and then everybody was untangling real fast like an octopus exploding, and Karen went over the side, down onto the floor, and I couldn't get it to go back down and inside my pants fast enough, and then I was being lifted up and jerked off the bed by the back of my pants, and Mr. Morris slapped me on the shoulder so hard I spun around and fell against a wicker wastebasket and broke it. He said, "You are not ladies and gentlemen." He wasn't happy. Karen didn't cry, she just looked sullen and furious, but somebody out in the hall was crying. I finally got my pants together and stood up, and my shoulder hurt from where that man hit me, and we all straggled down the stairs. Martin Kwalick said to me, "I think the party's over." He and I walked the first two blocks together, in the icy rain, and he gave me a couple of hits off his last number, and then we said later. I was almost home when I realized my wallet was missing. I panicked and said Jesus Christ, and staggered around in spaced confusion. What a fool! I started to go back, but then I figured that was not a cool move, and since my name was in it on a card, I would just wait. I didn't want to phone. Karen could call me or bring it to school on Monday. Which is the story of how I lost my wallet instead of my cherry.

I picked up the phone and there it was again, nothing. I was getting used to it. But this time there was a switch and a deep voice said, "Well, well." That's all, and then click. The cranks never stop. And now that our record rainfall was being followed by a record cold wave, I didn't like to stay in The Pink Fang because the 1921 furnace was not big enough for the job and I had to sit next to the little heater Dad bought at Sears and wait for the phone to ring. There were also suspicious things. We found the bottom of a woman's blue bathing suit sitting down there on the washing machine, and Dad didn't believe I knew nothing about it and I didn't believe he knew nothing about it, and all we needed was to have distrustfulness added to suspicion. We couldn't figure out at all what the bottom of a blue woman's bathing suit was doing popping up. It was very old, not a bikini, and frayed and had a stain in the crotch. Neither Dad nor I would bring a woman here in the dead of winter to leave an old-fashioned blue bottom of a bathing suit.

Nothing made sense. I came singing into the house on Saturday afternoon while Dad was at the studio and there in the sunroom, talking on our telephone, was Dexter. He hung up right away. I said, "What are you doing?"

He said, "Nothing." And he then walked around the hallway in his boots, stamp stamp stamp, scuffing the floor. I told him to cut it out, and he said, "You don't understand anything."

I pushed him, hard, and he shouted at me, "Your dad said I could come in any time I want to. He even gave me a key. *See?*" And he showed me a key, stuck it up into my face.

I was mixed up.

"When you were off in Hollywood, he and I had a good time." Dexter was very loud. "He might a-*dopt* me."

"Did he say that?"

Dexter sat on the bottom step, like he owned it, one eye closed and the other staring at the red glass Peace sign Dad had hung from the ceiling. Dexter said, "Blam!" pointing with his finger, like a gun.

"Did he say that?"

"Blam!" said Dexter.

The phone rang. I looked at it and then at Dexter. It rang two more times, and he said, "Well, aren't you going to answer it?" I said, "Why don't you?" He said, "It's not my phone." So I went to it and picked it up and said furiously, "Say something."

It was Karen Morris, she had found my wallet.

I tried to be calm, and she said she was calling from the extension—she was whispering—and she said it was pretty hairy at her house now, she couldn't get out, but she'd give me the wallet at school. She said her dad took the rubber out of it, and I'd even forgotten it was still in there, that rubber's been in there for at least a year, I got it way back in Syracuse, and it's probably all moldy. I groaned and I told Karen to stay rough and I'd see her at school. Then I threw Dexter out of the house and he stood on the porch kicking at the door, and I wasn't upstairs two minutes before he let himself in again with the key Dad gave him.

That night at dinner I said to Dad that he'd have to choose between me and Dexter. It was shitty, but I felt I had to. Dad was very confused and didn't tell me the whole truth, just a song and dance about how Dexter had been thrown 50 curve balls by life already and somebody had to give him some love and affection, with his parents abandoning him and his grandmother dying and his grandfather in a stupor. I said, "K, but you didn't have to give him a key to the house." Dad said he came home one day while Dylan and I were in Hollywood and found Dexter freezing and soaking wet outside and his own house was locked, so Dad gave him the key for emergencies. Maybe so, but as we sat there over our steaks, I just thought to myself that those 4 days when his two sons were gone must have been a very lonely time for Dad, a real blow, and he must have felt like a total failure, probably on the edge of suicide, so he latched onto Dexter as a safety valve. I said, "Are you going to adopt him?"

Dad smiled sadly. "No, Jacky, I have no plans to adopt Dexter."

"He thinks you do."

Dad just sighed.

Which somehow in my mind is connected to my stealing the car. I didn't really steal it, but I had been thinking of borrowing it for some time. Dad had given me lessons, and he let me drive it for a few miles at Point Reyes, which was a thrill, and up in the Oakland hills when he was beside me as my teacher. So on Sunday when he got tanked up watching the Raiders' game in San Diego and crashed—"I'm going to take a little nap, Jacky, K?" and I know those "little" naps, they can go for 3 hours— I said K, and waited until the snoring and then took the yellow foam rubber pillow that Dylan always used to eat on in the dining room, and my beret, which I put on to shield the upper part of my face, and left a note: "Dad, Went for a spin, Home soon, Jack The Bear," and it was a hard cold rain so with windshield wipers and all there would be poor visibility, and I wouldn't get caught—although since I was minus my wallet, if I was pulled over, it would be curtains, and I got the seat up real close, and backed out of the driveway, between Mr. Mitchell's old camper on my left and Norman's dead-as-a-doornail T-Bird, and then I was off on my adventure in the Swinger. I drove carefully and put the radio on full volume to some Soulful Sounds, and I went doom-doom-de-doom-doom and just didn't give a shit, the All-American Boy Car Thief.

My first brush with the law was on Grand Avenue, where they had set up one of those Vehicle Inspections, but luckily I saw it in time and pulled into the Safeway parking lot just where Dad had that little wreck, and I was panting with fear, but I made it, and as I was waiting for a guy to back out of a space he went too far and bumped into the rear of a parked car, slightly, and there was a woman in that parked car and she honked and the driver of the other car, a big old Buick, went on about six feet and then stopped. I zipped into his place and got out and started to walk away, because the cops might be on my tail for that illegal turn, but then I got interested in the argument. The woman, who was white, got out of her car and said, "I was sitting here reading a letter and you bumped into my car." The driver of the Buick, who was black and very old, seemed confused, and he said, "I didn't bump yoah cah, I alwas look when ahm backin up." The woman was fragile, I guess you could say she was *dainty* or *petite*, and she said, "I beg your pardon," very soft-spoken and kind of ducking her chin, "but I felt you hit." The old black guy looked at her fender and there was no damage, he must have hit on the bumper, but I know he actually did hit her because her car jiggled. He said, "They's no marks on yoah cah, I didn't come this close to yoah cah," and he held out his hands about 2 feet apart. She, the woman, was looking, and she couldn't see marks, so she said, "Well, as long as there's no damage," and he just got all huffy-puffy in the rain and said to the world, "Shyyeeit, I din' come close to that woman's cah, crazy people blamin' you all the time," and he said a few more shyyeeits as he went back to the Buick, and the woman was shy and in the right and I would have said something except for, (1) there was no damage, and (2) he was black, and (3), mainly, I was a car thief and my word would not be believed and I'd have to explain. So I hung around in the Safeway parking lot getting wet until everything blew over except the rain, and then I got behind the wheel and looked *very* carefully as I was backing up, and continued my merry way.

The next adventure was twenty minutes later, after I circled Lake Merritt and then went up Broadway and cut onto College Avenue, heading toward Berkeley to pick up some Zig-Zag papers, and I saw this chick in the pouring rain, hitchhiking, and she was very pregnant, in a black cape, and her blond hair was soaked and so I pulled over.

She jumped in, smelling like a wet girl, she must have been only about 19, and she said, "Wow, thanks."

I said, "Where you headed?"

Then she looked at me. She said, "Hey, man, you're a kid."

I looked at her. I was scared.

She said, "Up there, it's on Woolsey, I'll show you."

"K," I said.

She said, "It's really a nice car," and she put her hands on the padded dash, and the seat belt warning sign on the instrument panel was a red light in my brain but I

173

couldn't ask her to buckle up for safety because she was so pregnant and maybe the belt wasn't even long enough.

She said, "Did you steal it?"

I said, "It's my dad's car."

She said oh.

We drove.

She said, "It was really nice to pick me up, I was *drowning*. I'm sorry I said you were a kid."

"Well," I said, "you have to call a spade a spade."

She said, "Honey, you ain't no spade."

And we laughed, it was K now. We understood each other. I thought of asking her if she wanted to stop at a drive-in, for a pickle milk shake, or something dumb-ass clever like that, and she said she was really tired, she was in her 10th month, the baby was sposed to come by Halloween. She pointed out Woolsey, and we could barely see because of the downpour, hail now, and she said she was Snow White and lived with the 7 Dwarfs, and she did, 7 guys and her, all in one house. She said they were really fine far-out guys, and she cooked for them, and they were preparing a Delivery Party, for when she gave birth, and they were all going to take acid and one guy was going to film it. That's Berkeley. She said I was sweet to take on a pregnant pickup, and invited me in for some Jasmine Tea, but I said I better be going. She got out, and slammed the door, and I started to take off like Dudley Studly, floorboarding it, and then she screamed and what she had done was shut the door on her black cape, and she was running beside the car and I jammed on the brakes and she fell—if I just had had more experience with cars I would have known to slow down gradually, but like a little idiot I stood on the brakes, and then I cut the motor and tore out of the car, around the front, and she was lying there, gasping, and I opened the door where her cape was caught, and helped her into the house where

3 of the dwarfs who were really tall were lounging around watching TV and we explained, and she had some tea, and after 15 minutes we decided she was all right. She said it was her fault because she slammed the door on her cape, but I knew whose fault it always is. One of the guys, Jeffrey, wanted to call the doctor but she said no. She went upstairs to wash the blood off her knees. She had leaves and mud on her cape. I can't believe how suave I am.

I was too shaken to continue my car-stealing act, so I tooled home in a daze, supercareful for cops, and Dad was still down, so I tore up the note I had left and took a bath. I was up to my ears in hot water, thinking suicide was too good for me, when Dad stumbled in and said, "What's new?"

And as a perfect ending to a perfect day, that very night was the all-time mind blower, the complete freak-out when I lost my mind.

We had another anonymous phone call just for openers, and then Dad and I went out for another Roundtable Authentic Early English pizza and I had forgotten to return the seat to its original position, which Dad noticed, and it made me awkward for a second—at least I didn't leave the fucking yellow foam rubber pillow in there, I'm a total fool but I'm not stupid—and he let me order the pizza the way I like it, "Merlin's Marvel," with mushroom and sausage and olives. And then we came home and he seemed to be inching back to his old self, and he had another joint to clear his head and we played 3 games of ping-pong, which I took 2 games to 1, and then we turned the house into total darkness and had a round of the old flashlight game. He played "Dragon's Desire," which is another Roundtable pizza, and I'd scoot from dining room to sunroom as I watched the crazy angles of the beam as he tried to get hold of me. I practically killed myself in the sunroom because I forgot about that half cord of wood he had ordered when the cold spell hit, and we had spent two hours bringing it in from where the kid dumped it off the truck onto the sidewalk, and it doesn't burn very well and Dad said he got a double hernia hauling it in, while I helped, but now we had a double row of logs all around the sun porch, which I forgot, and crashed into it and almost went through the french windows. I said, "Mother-fucker shit"—and far away upstairs Dad said, "Do I hear the pitter-patter of little dirty words?" I saved myself by my false alarms, ping-pong balls, that I'd lob to wrong rooms like hand grenades so that he would be deceived. He was muttering, "Ping-pong, King Kong," like a robot lie detector, and I was trying not to giggle or give myself away. It was just like hairy old times, so I sneaked up the stairs and down the stairs and into my lady's chamber. I was feeling like a carefree kid again. Dad was saying in a closet, "Lost, lost, in an impenetrable forest," and I sneaked down the stairs again all the way into his Growlery. I pushed the bell by the door that the crippled lady had used so many years ago, and I could still hear Dad going, "Ho-Ho-Ho," like Sandy Claws way upstairs, in the North Pole, it was cold enough, and pressing the bell in his room, and then suddenly there was another bell somewhere else, and I stopped short to listen. Dad might not even have heard it, spaced out like he was. I pressed mine again, and so did he up there, and then so did whoever else was in the house, the cold Pink Fang, where the temperature during the day was only 58°.

It was even colder than that in the basement, and so was I. I was frozen, and I said first to myself that I was imagining things again, but I knew I wasn't. There were *three* people in the blacked-out house. Then I told myself it was only Dexter, who had his own personal key, and he loves to ring bells. I held my breath. I crawled down beside the furnace where the P. G. & E. man came that day to look for leaks, and then I crawled back to the bottom of the basement stairs. Dad let out a shout, and then there was silence and a dim leftover of light was on the walls in the front hallway, I could see it from down there where I was. I could hear them talking. I wanted to hide myself in the dirt behind the furnace, where Dad said the bodies were buried in the Panama Canal, but I was freezing more and more and I could hear them talking, whispering. It was not in my mind. They were really talking.

I almost passed out right there when Dad screamed. He had been saying, "It's all right now," and then, "It's going to be all right," and then something went all wrong, and terrible, and Dad screamed. You knew right away it wasn't like on Thriller or Creature's Features, he was hurt. He was hurt in deep pain, and I could hear footsteps and shoving up there, in the dark, and falling down, and I was trapped at the door of the Growlery. I waited, holding out my hands and shaking like a leaf and sick so bad that the pizza would probably gangway up out of my gut all over the wall, and there was a crash up there on the stairs and I could hear pieces of wood splitting which was the banister rails getting smashed. Dad had thrown a body right through it. And then he screamed again, sort of like being hurt and also like Tarzan or something when he kills, but it was too desperate for that shit, it was not the movies or the end of the world, it was being *hurt*. Dad screamed again like he'd been hurt so much he could never again live a normal life. King's X, or Call It Off On Account of Darkness, or That's Enough, or *any*thing. I ran to the cellar back door leading into Monster Gardens, and flipped the latch, and I started to escape into the ivy and all that running-wild undergrowth, but I stopped because Dad was screaming to wake up the dead and something was still going on and it made me so vomity that I couldn't run away and be a coward, and run out on him when he needed me, especially since I came back for that purpose. I remembered that piece from the half cord of wood that wasn't too big and we had used it to retrieve ping-pong balls when Dad slammed them under the tool chest. So I got it where we left it, on top of the suitcase, and I held it, and then I could hear an awful spitting and Dad's murmuring choked half words and his voice and then the other voice saying, "Well, well," in the echo chamber of the basement stairs, and the footsteps came down slowly like on shoes filled with lead, and I held onto my trusty piece of wood, and just when that fucking monster got down to the bottom holding out the flashlight that he had taken away from Dad I curled with all my might for a home run and I let him have it, I smashed at his face with the firewood with my eyes closed, and he fell to the floor with the flashlight skidding and bouncing and rolling away from him.

It was Dad covered with blood. I opened my eyes and I saw him with my mind ripping at a thousand miles per hour, and he was just poor creamed Dad, cut on the face and sliced up and blood oozing, and then at the top of the stairs to the basement that voice said again, "Well, well." I duck-walked over to the flashlight and pointed it up there and at first I didn't believe it was him, even though I knew all along it had to be, because of his disguise—the beard which was not a freaky-far-out beard of a hippie but very neat and clipped and planned. Norman, with the knife he had used to slash up Dad. Behind me and sort of under me Dad moaned, and one of my feet was on his shoulder.

I dimly had a vision from far away about my plans when Norman made his move on Dylan, how I would say I poisoned Cheyenne, but Dad was leaking blood and unconscious, twitching on the freezing floor, and now Norman himself was coming down slowly to finish the job. I got off Dad's shoulder with my one foot and I said to myself this was supposed to take place outdoors in my mind where I could run away and have the advantage, and it was Dylan, not Dad, but now it was so freezing damp in the cellar. I saw what I had to do, and I shouted up at Norman, holding the flashlight on his face, that gray color, "You have nigger blood in you—your dad told my dad, it's your family secret that nobody tells, your mother isn't really your mother, she was a *nigger*," because I remembered Norman's hatred of black people.

Norman stopped and was speechless. He didn't even say, "Well, well."

I said, "Your dad *confessed*. Your mother is a nigger."

It worked. Norman started to move fast, and so did I, out the back door that I had already unlocked in my panic. I shouted to the freezing night, "Norman is a nigger, *Norman's mother is a nigger*." I would have thrown up, but I didn't have time for it, I was running a down-and-out pass pattern, crying and sick, so sick my brain felt like it was bleeding, and Norman was limping along on his bad leg, and I saw the noble tree, wet and frosted and blowing now in the cold wave, it was unbelievable and so huge like in a dream, and I pulled myself up onto the lowest limb on the plank that was propped up there years ago, and I kept on screaming. I turned and saw him coming after me, with the knife, and I screamed, "Nigger, *nigger*, NIGGER—" and I was out of my mind, which woke up the Dobermans, and they whined and barked and fishtailed around jumping.

Norman pulled himself up into our noble tree, and I was frozen to my bones not to mention completely mind-fucked, and I hauled myself up to a long mossy frozen-solid limb, and I pulled myself out onto it, still screaming, like I was retarded with my racist philosophy, to the wind without mercy. All I could think was Get Norman Away From Dad. Norman sliced his hand on his own knife as he was climbing on ice-wood, and he dropped the knife, and then I knew he'd just have to get me with his bare hands and strangle me, so I moved farther out and got hold of a limb above, and then I jumped up and down on the limb I was standing on to try to shake him off, but he had hold, and I looked down and got sick again while the wind was tearing through me like nights in Syracuse in February. Norman felt sick too, but hatred is stronger than that any day, or night, even if it's freezing, and Norman stepped out after me, and I was at the end of my rope, or limb, and there was another one I could swing to, in that noble tree, if I kept in mind my acrobat training from Dad, who was bleeding to death at the door of his Growlery, and so I said with my eyes to Norman, Come on and kill me, and he tried, he lunged, and I made my leap and missed with my left hand but held on with the right, like a thousand needles into my hand but I had no choice, and the limb whipped a recoil and Norman fell into the Dobermans. I thought he had to break his back at that point, because it was fifteen or twenty feet down, on the slant of the hill, and the ground was frozen. I got my left hand back up, and then I pulled myself up over and almost punctured my lung on a knot, tearing my shirt and belly inside, my hand was bleeding as I swung around and slapped myself in the face by accident, I didn't know what I was doing except by reflex and fear. I screamed like a baby, "HELP, HELP, HELP." I could see even when I was screaming that Norman, who was supposed to have broken his back, was up on his feet again and stumbling through the yard down there with the Dobermans munching and freaking and hanging onto his clothes, biting and tearing at him, and later in my dreams I was reminded of that scene in *The Thing* when Our Visitor from Outer Space plunges off into the snow with the dogs all over him, and Norman was screaming like The Thing, as anyone would do who was being chewed and eaten alive by Dobermans, especially when he had planned it all to be calm, as he probably did, and I backed down toward the trunk of the tree while lights were coming on in that house where the owners of the Dobermans live, and lights coming on at the Mitchell house. I knew help had to be on its way. I was still out of my head, and on a simple drop back to the ground of no more than six feet I landed on the iced-up leaves and my feet went out from under me, and I tried to break my fall with my arm—only I broke my arm instead of my fall. It happened so fast, the pain was green and icy in my head. I carried my arm like a package, crying and screaming, as I ran back up inside to dial O with my good hand in the sunroom, and have an epileptic fit in front of the operator, and then run to the door to answer the bell, and it was Dexter's father, grandfather—Mr. Mitchell the Seabee—who was monsterish in his eyes and face, but I just pointed downstairs with my broken arm's elbow, it was killing me, and he found Dad soaked in blood.

Mr. Mitchell had already called the police, because he heard the screaming, and he started first aid after he found the light switch. He tore off his own shirt to use it, and tore pieces of it for the blood. He kept saying, "Oh, Jesus, oh, Jesus," over and over again. But by this time I was not in my right mind, and all I knew was that I never wanted to fall asleep again because my dreams wouldn't shut off if I live to be 100. After Mr. Mitchell got Dad on the couch he made a splint for my arm out of magazines, and I was babbling in my mind, flashing all over the place, and finally when the ambulance came I should have relaxed and instead I made a fool of myself, shouting everything, the dirtiest words any child ever heard of, like cocksucker turd lover shit fuck cunt. I was so cold and shaking.

That night when I woke up in the soft blue-green light of the hospital it was all medicine and anesthetic. I puked totally in my mind and some on the pillow.

Dad lost an unbelievable amount of blood, and he'll have some permanent scars because they had to take over forty stitches. I am stuck with this fucking cast on my arm, but it isn't serious, it was just a "green stick break of the wrist." Dad had to answer questions in the hospital, and the Leary Boys, a Father and Son act, were back in the news, another chapter in the Monster Drama in the East Bay. I had dreams coming out of the anesthetic groggy in electric orbit that Dad was saying to me, "I'm proud of you, Jack The Bear, you did what I trained you to do, you performed your duty," but that's just me and fantasy again, he never said a thing like that. He was too hurt and in shock. I still have a weak spot for him in spite of everything. He didn't speak for 24 hours, he just looked at me, and he had to have the transfusions, and I will outgrow my nonsense of heroic dreams someday and accept life. You can't be Bongo The Bear on your unicycle forever.

I was with him, in his room, when he got the call from

Grandma and Grandpa. She said, "When will it ever end?" and I said I didn't know. I apologized about stealing the 2 $20 bills, and she told me to forget that nonsense and get well and was I in pain? Dylan did not come to the phone, but he was all right and happy and never needed to know about this. Then Dad and Grandpa talked, and I stared out the hospital window at the lights of Oakland.

Dad slept, his face covered with bandages. I watched TV in the lounge, until curfew, and had a good talk with a guy who got a septic tank on his leg and crushed it. He showed me his tattoos, from the Navy, and I thought of Mr. Mitchell in the Seabees. But that made me think of Dexter, which I did in the privacy of my room—semi-private because there was another kid in there, who had an emergency job on his appendix—and I decided in the green-blue light that there are things I will never be able to forgive and forget, I sound just like Grandpa. Dad would say it's not Dexter's fault, because Norman had complete power over him and used him as his personal robot, for information and getting the key and dumb shit like the blue bathing suit bottom, and even if life did throw Dexter 50 curves I know I should hope for the best for him but he almost got us all killed. If Norman scared Dexter shitless Norman scared me supershitless and could have destroyed my whole life, not to mention Dylan and Dad, and I was pretty sure he has destroyed a lot of it anyway, so I hope Dexter has the long unhappy life he so richly deserves. It's what I feel, without explanation or apology.

I know more than I want to about Dad, and his contribution. We didn't find out until later how Norman got away and laid low after he abandoned his stolen rented car. He made it all the way to Arizona, and the authorities couldn't follow his zig-zag trail, which probably wasn't planned to be complicated since Norman's not exactly a genius at planning. But he got lonely for the parents he hates, and so he finally made his way back to good old Oakland, and his mother and father loved him in spite of everything, he was their only child, and they wanted to protect him. Besides he hadn't really killed anybody, he did let Dylan go. So they hid him in the house. But one night Dad saw Norman in a careless moment, at that front window where the lamp is, and Dad was plastered again and he suddenly went berserk and didn't call the police, which he would have done sober, and he ran over there himself, with our fucking broom. He isn't really to blame, I guess, because it's a natural reaction, but when he couldn't get an answer at the door or anything he smashed their window with that broom, and went in through it, and rampaged around to catch Norman, who by that time escaped. But Dad did a lot of damage to the house, he must have been totally bombed, breaking all sorts of stuff, even china and pictures. I myself have used that broom a few times, to sweep in the kitchen, and once we jousted with it. I don't know, all I know is Dad went crazy, and didn't even call the police until the next day when he calmed down. I wasn't there, I was in Hollywood.

But when I ran away and came back, he could have told me, even if he was thinking he didn't want to frighten me needlessly. *He should have told me.*

And it enraged Norman, who was always pretty fucking enraged anyway, Dad busting up his own parents' house and trying to get him. Smashing the window, and all that hairy booze crap. Dad's blitz got Norman boiling again.

I suppose Dad was ashamed, which is also a reason for not telling me about it. I guess he had just been through too much, and he snapped, he couldn't hold it all in his mind. I don't even want to know the details, although they fascinate me. At least I know now why he said that

186

time that his heart was beginning to beat with the monster's heart.

I could have handled it, I really could have, if he'd told me.

So after a few days he and I went down and spent the week in Hollywood again, and there were lots of discussions and bad scenes, but now Dylan and Dad and I are back here once again in our Oakland house—we've stopped calling it The Pink Fang—and Dad wrote a letter to Syracuse, inquiring about getting his old job back. We've had about enough California for a while. But the answer letter from Channel 44 must not have been encouraging, because I saw it in the mail and put it with the magazines on the dining table, and waited, and when Dad read it he crumpled it up and threw it in the fireplace. And he's not doing too well at Channel 2, either —he says they're "carrying" him. Peg Edinger comes over sometimes, and I don't know what we'd do without her, she is a tremendous person, but maybe we're too far gone even for her to help. Dad just stares at the long afternoons, and I watch him when I get home from school. I myself probably will grow up and have children and mess up life, except I make a solemn promise I won't, once is enough. I do want to keep the spirit my dad once had. After all is said and done, he had *spirit*. And gave it to me. For example, Norman would probably have killed me if I didn't have the acrobatic training from Dad, so I could catch that limb in the noble tree. Dad is something else.

But he broke down and actually telephoned a "shrink" for an interview. Include me, maybe "shrinks" have family plans, like airlines. Dylan is the one who is doing the best, and he was the one who got kidnapped and ate dirt and almost died in the rain at night. But he's getting his sunny disposition back. He'll never remember the gruesome details. Or maybe he will. I still haven't lost my cherry—and probably won't, because the Morrises are really moving to San Jose and Karen spends days at a time down there with her mother, never thinking of me. But I would like to lose it, I want it to be done, a clean-stick break and not a green-stick break, maybe I'll just go to a whore and do it, if I can recognize one, which I think I can.

It's been weeks now, since the shit-storm, and by January 5 I'll have the cast on my arm completely off. At Christmas Dylan got a Fisher-Price garage which he plays with all the time, and I got a guitar which I can work on privately as soon as the old arm heals. I got Dad a rust-colored turtleneck, $15. But we are in bad shape. Throw out the life line, throw out the life line, someone is drifting away. Dad pulls that rust-colored turtleneck up over his head and watches the TV through it. He never drinks or blows dope now, and won't go near it, but it's almost worse, the way he holds himself like someone's about to smash him at any moment.

If he has learned his lesson he has nothing to show for it. At a certain point you can't work up the energy to stage a comeback. It's like he was in a war somewhere. Every once in a while Mr. Wonderful peeps out again, mainly in games, and I see it, and that only makes it worse because mainly he's Dr. Gloom. I would do any-thing in my power, but power is what I don't have. I see his face twitch. He won't give you an honest answer. And he sees all too clearly how my feelings are chang-ing, and even when I try to fake it and cover up, he sees. It drives him crazy into his corner. And sometimes I say vicious things, in spite of myself. He loses hope. He can't look anyone in the eye. And he comes up with sugges-tions that are so weird. Like on Saturday, he wanted to go *bowling*. He and I would bowl, and Dylan could horse around watching. Bowling?

I have my cast on my left arm, and I'm a rightie, but

188

the cast screwed up my timing, though I wouldn't use it as an excuse. We were fools, at the U-BOWL, and we both sent a lot of balls into the gutter, it is a down sport. And Dylan tried to be happy, but he really wasn't, and got bored and wandered into people's ways. We could just go back to the basement and play ping-pong, except we can't. We've got to get out of that house, even if Norman isn't a threat any more, because they locked up what the Dobermans left of him. But on the other hand we can't keep on running away from bad memories. I saw a poster in Berkeley that said, WHAT HAS REALITY DONE FOR YOU LATELY? And I started to point it out to Dad, but you have to be careful with him now. After we bowled, the three of us had Cokes, and he mentioned a Saturday movie matinee, which we were obviously too late for. "Jacky Bear," he said to me, "we've got to change."

I let it pass. He's hurting so bad, and I can't kick him when he's down. So why do I do it silently, with my eyes, when I know he can tell? I should support him. I entered an art contest, because I thought a blue ribbon might cheer him up, but I got Honorable Mention and that's not It. I just play it by ear, and try to let him talk to me when he needs to. But in the U-BOWL he wasn't talking, and I waited there staring at the ice in the bottom of the Coke plastic glass, and I was seeing the stitch marks on his face without even looking at them, and I knew we'd never be the way we used to be, and I don't even care. Except I care completely, if not more. I hate growing up. I said, "Gotta pee," and I went into the MEN'S and stood around and leaked right on the floor for spite, and then came out.

He said, "Boys, let's get out of this blind alley."

Dylan wanted a candy, so we got him one, a mint at the cash register.

Dad said in the car, right in front of Dylan in the back

seat, to me in the front, "You don't love me the old way, do you?"

I can't stand all this unbearable shit. I said, "You must be pretty insensitive if that's what you think."

He mumbled something like a sigh. He couldn't even play at being sarcastic, which is our last chance.

I looked at the nothing East Bay day going by, and I didn't say anything else. What I wanted to say was YOU'VE GOT TO BE KIDDING. That's my choice for what they write on my tombstone.

At home, in the driveway, we were piling out of the car, and Dad never likes for Dylan to get his sneakers soaked on the grass after a rain, and I got out, and then Dylan jumped out onto the lawn when I held the seat forward, and Dad shouted, "NO!" Scared the poor little guy.

Dad can't react any more. He bolted out and swooped Dylan up, and Dylan said, "NO!" He was on the edge of tears, and he hit Dad on the face, like he used to do in fun, but his fist hit a scar place, and Dad swatted him with a free hand, holding him in the other one, a swat on the top of the butt, and then Dylan went over the edge into bawling.

I watched it. And Dad was lost in our own front yard, he wanted to discipline and he wanted to be fair and he just wanted all the hurting to stop. But it's a perfect example of how he can't handle shit any more. Dylan blubbered, and it killed my father, it killed him.

"I just mean," Dad said to the boy in his arms, "you shouldn't ever hit anybody in the face, K?"

Dylan couldn't say K. He was crying.

All over getting some fucking sneakers wet, which we could have changed the minute we got in the door.

"Daddy didn't mean to scare you, son, he was just worried about you." Dad was clutching him too hard.

Dylan, still bawling, said, "Daddy don't do that." And then Dad put him down, very slowly, and then Dad fell down there onto the wet grass, collapsing in slow motion for the count of 10.

I didn't bend down. I stood there beside him. I said, "Get up."

On his back he looked at me, his eyes blinking. He said, "I plunged through those french doors. Headfirst." The cold was all over him, and his arm pointed toward our house and the glass of the french doors.

I looked there. And then I looked up across the street at Norman's house. And I saw in my mind Dad somewhere breaking through glass, in slow motion, like in a movie, Dad just coming at me and the pieces of window glass spraying away. But then I tried not to do that, and I saw him real, messed up on the grass of our own yard.

Here Lies Marcus Superfluous.

Then I did bend down, and I carefully picked out those pieces of glass that didn't even exist, in Dad's hair. I said to him, "I think I got it all."

Dad waited, and sat up, and got on his feet again. He said, "Thanks." He brushed the frozen water off his pants and the sleeves of his jacket.

I said to the world, God help us. I have had enough. Too much shit for me.

Dad picked up Dylan again, being very gentle this time with his little guy, and Dylan looked at him, and said, worried, "Daddy got wet?"

Dad said, walking up to the porch, "Yeah—Daddy got wet."

I tagged along behind them into the house. And those tears of course, fighting them. I've got to be a man. The summer I reach sixteen, I'm going to Europe, and that's final, Scout's fucking honor.